THE ACE OF ASSASSINS

Nigel Wigmore

Cover design by Benjamin Wigmore
All rights reserved, Copyright © Nigel Wigmore 2024.
browsingimpala publishing
ISBN: 9798327123021

"The race is not always to the swift, nor the battle to the strong,
but that's the way to bet."
Damon Runyon

For Ben

2003

Chapter 1

LONDON, August, and it was hot. A short, wiry guy in a red jacket was in a hurry. He threaded his way through the dull commuter crowd. His name was Little Frankie Roseo - New York hitman on vacation.

In the Tube, Little Frankie rounded a corner of a white-tiled tunnel and heard music, Procol Harum's, A Whiter Shade of Pale, played by an orchestra. Or so it seemed.

He wheeled through a further bend, taking quick steps, and there was a busker, squatting on his hams with a tiny, ancient synthesiser in his lap. Here was your orchestra.

Little Frankie stopped and stood a while, watching. The busker, oblivious, pumped up the music. People filed by. Little Frankie reached into his red sports jacket and brought out his roll. He peeled off an English £20 note from a large wad.

He put his wad away, stepped forward and dropped the note onto the busker's spread-out, mouldy leather jacket. It was already dotted with small change.

The music wavered and almost stumbled, then jangled on.

Little Frankie leaned forward so he was close to the busker, who was just a kid.

"Hey, kid," Little Frankie said. "You made my day."

The busker glanced up at Little Frankie with big moon, doped-up eyes. There was a tiny flicker of gratitude or maybe there was nothing. Without taking his eyes off Little Frankie, the busker snaked out a hand, snatched the precious note and stashed it in a safe place.

"And I guess I made yours," Little Frankie said, turning and walking away. Little Frankie resumed his Tube journey at a more leisurely pace. He wanted to take in the London Underground scene, something new to him.

He exited the Underground at Tottenham Court Road station. He stood on the pavement's edge near the Dominion Theatre. He was waiting for something or someone.

Little Frankie was in his fifties, with a dark complexion and tough, black hair, greying at the temples. Everyone back home in Brooklyn always said he had style. Today, on vacation in London, he wore a seventy-dollar T-shirt by Shadows, $350 George Marciano cotton-denim jeans, and Armani suede bucks at $700 a throw. His red jacket was no ordinary sports coat. It cost him $4,500 in SoHo, New York and was a Versace. Little Frankie would be happy to tell anyone this. But only if they asked because Little Frankie was modest to a fault.

Charing Cross Road towards Cambridge Circus bubbled in the mid-summer heat, the hottest on record. In the distance, a vermilion red Bentley Continental with the top down snatched its way through the patchy traffic.

By the time the Bentley was within 50 yards of Little Frankie, it was noticeable. People were staring. So was Little Frankie. Especially when the Bentley slewed towards him.

"What the fu . . ?"

The Bentley mounted the pavement a few feet from where he stood. People scattered but Little Frankie did not move. The Bentley jerked to a halt in front of him. A red-haired man dived out, slapped a big Jiffy Bag in Little Frankie's hands then dived back into the Bentley.

The red-haired guy smoked the tyres all the way up Charing Cross Road. Little Frankie turned away.

"Draw attention to yourself, pal," he muttered. "I'm gone."

Little Frankie hailed a black cab. He was in luck. One stopped right away. And, like the red-haired guy in the Bentley, Little Frankie disappeared.

He sat in the middle of the back seat of the cab, the big Jiffy Bag in his lap.

"Drive around the park, will ya, pal," he said.

The cabbie shrugged and slipped the cab's glass partition shut. Little Frankie sat back and opened the Jiffy Bag. Inside there were two envelopes. One was large and fat, the other one thin and small.

Little Frankie opened the fat one first. It smelled of money. He peeped inside. Then out again, quick, as if whatever was in there might bite him.

"Jesus!" he said out loud.

The cabbie flung back the partition.

"Do what, guv?"

"Keep driving, will ya."

The cabbie shrugged once more and again flung the partition shut.

Little Frankie stared at the fat envelope. He tucked it back inside the Jiffy Bag and turned his attention to the small envelope. He opened it. It contained a single sheet of paper with a name typewritten on it.

"What the hell? Hey, cabbie! Pull over, will ya! Lemme out!"

Chapter 2

LITTLE Frankie had jumped out of the cab at Hyde Park Corner. He stood for a while, collecting his thoughts. Calmer, he made a call from his phone to an old friend, Mikey O'Callaghan, who lived and worked in London.

"Is that really you, Frankie? In London? I can hardly believe it," Mikey O'Callaghan said with a chuckle.

"What can I say, Mikey? I am right here in London, England!"

"But, Frankie, you never leave New York."

"Huh, I was in Miami, coupla times."

"Yeah?"

"And I am in Vegas, sometime."

"No kidding?"

"When we were kids," Little Frankie said. "You were always the kidder, Mikey."

"So, you are here on vacation?"

"Yeah. But something comes up. Can we meet?"

"Sure. Where are you?"

"In the park, I guess."

"There's this pasta joint. Duke Street, off Oxford Street. Get a cab. Meet me there in fifteen." Later in the restaurant, Little Frankie and Mikey O'Callaghan sat down at a table in a booth opposite one another. It was mid-morning, and the place was quiet.

Little Frankie sipped a double espresso while Mikey buried his chops in a fluffy cappuccino and a monster Danish. Mikey was overweight, smoked too much, and was a guy's sort of guy. The big Jiffy Bag had been placed by Little Frankie on a chair between them.

"Things are changing, Mikey. Things I cannot believe."

"9/11?"

"Yeah, it was like the end of the world. Uh, people say it changed everything. I know a lot of people have said that. I know some people don't think so. Me, I think it has changed things. Some people think the shock has worn off. But not for me, Mikey, you understand what I'm saying? I am still in shock. Because I know I could turn on the TV tomorrow and hear that a nuclear bomb has gone off in New York City."

Mikey stopped munching and stared at his friend.

"It's these terrorists, Mikey."

"Yeah?"

"They are everywhere."

"Sure."

"Nearly 3,000 people died, Mikey. In one hit. Jesus!"

Little Frankie sipped his espresso.

"D'you mind me asking what you're doing in London, Frankie?"

"Like I said, I am on vacation."

"And . . ?"

"And? I like to work. You know I like to work."

Mikey stared at his old friend.

"Jesus, a hit! You're here for a hit?"

"Not so loud, huh. It's no big deal. It's routine. Or it was."

"Was?"

"Yeah, it was but it is no longer. My boss he has this cousin. In a place called Clerkenwell – you know it?" Mikey nodded and took another bite of Danish. "It's a favour, nothing more. I agree a small fee. When I get here, I am offered one half mil!"

"Half a million bucks! Christ, Frankie, who do they want you to waste, the Queen of England?"

"I have ten grand in this Jiffy Bag, right now."

"You're walking around London with ten thousand dollars in a Jiffy Bag?"

"Pounds, Mikey. That's your English pounds. This is a down payment. I get the rest when I complete the job. Then I get some people to clean it up from here in London. Y'know, turn it into dollars."

Mikey munched furiously on the remains of his Danish. Little Frankie reached into the Jiffy Bag and pulled out the small envelope. He opened it and took out the single sheet of paper and placed it in front of O'Callaghan.

"Choke on this, Mikey: this is the hit!"

Mikey lifted the spectacles he kept dangling old-guy style from a red cord around his neck and pushed them slowly up his nose into position. He unfolded the sheet of paper and read the typewritten name.

His spectacles dropped from his nose and plummeted onto his chest. He re-folded the piece of paper and shoved it back across the table towards Little Frankie.

"The American ambassador?" Mikey said in a hoarse whisper. "They want you to hit the American ambassador! Are these guys nuts?"

Little Frankie put the piece of paper back inside the small envelope, which he placed back inside the Jiffy Bag.

"So, what do you think?"

"What do I think? What do I think? I think you give these people back the dough they have already given you. Then you high tail it back to New York as if nothing has happened. Frankie, whatever you do in your line of business, which, I have always said is entirely your business, this is not it. This is terrorism, for chrissakes!"

"Yeah, Mikey, that's how I figure it. Like a lot of people, I have spent the last few years trying to get over what happened in New York. I come to London on my first ever vacation here. I agree to do some work while I am here because that is what I do. I figure it is no big deal. I think it is some small job and I am not looking for trouble. But you know what, Mikey . . ."

"What, Frankie?"

"This is not going to happen, I swear to God! Whatever this is about, whoever puts me up to this, whoever these people are, I am not going to do it! More than that: I am gonna stop it happening."

Chapter 3

LITTLE Frankie paid off a cab and entered a cafe that had seen better days. The wire mesh security screens on its windows were a permanent, rusty fixture. The cafe was one of many similar small Italian establishments in this part of Clerkenwell, an area of London known as Little Italy.

It was mid-afternoon and the place was empty except for a woman cleaning up behind the downstairs take-out counter.

Her name was Natalie Scallion, only daughter of the owner, Mario Scallion, a double cousin of Sal Savoria, Little Frankie's boss. Natalie had a round, care-worn face, and a wary smile.

"Yes, what would you like?"

"Is Mario here?"

"My father? He's upstairs in the restaurant. But I'm sorry, it's closed."

"It's all right. He's expecting me. Frank Roseo, from New York City."

Natalie thought about this for a moment. Little Frankie waited.

"Go right up. He's in the kitchen." Little Frankie climbed the stairs into a medium-sized restaurant that was very workaday, and markedly Anglo-Italian. Large cheap frescoes depicting corny Italian/Venetian scenes decorated the walls. From a small kitchen in a corner of the room came the sound of pots clanging.

He went into the kitchen through a doorway separated from the restaurant by a cheap, beaded curtain. An old man with a drooping white moustache and flowing white hair was noisily washing up. This was Mario Scallion; the man Little Frankie had come to see.

"Mario?"

Mario turned around at the sound of Little Frankie's voice. He stopped what he was doing, and came slowly towards the hitman, peering at him shortsightedly and wiping his hands on his apron.

"Do I know you?"

"Sal sent me."

Mario stopped dead in his tracks. He stood motionless, staring in disbelief at Little Frankie.

"But why, why are you here?"

"Why am I here, Mario? Why am I here? You have no idea what you've gotten yourself into?"

Mario threw up his hands in exasperation, ripped off his apron, hurried out of the kitchen and rushed downstairs. Little Frankie followed him.

When he arrived downstairs, Mario was standing impassively behind the take-out counter. Natalie was nearby wiping tables. Little Frankie approached Mario.

"I figure, Mario, that you don't even know the name of the hit, do you?"

"There was no need," Mario said dismissively.

"Sal believed you Mario, when you said this was some routine job he was going to take care of for you, on your behalf. Because you are family."

Natalie stopped what she was doing and stared at Little Frankie.

"But this is not the case, is it Mario?"

"Why can't you do what they ask?" Mario pleaded, tears welling up in his old, rheumy eyes. "You agreed a contract! Sal said he would take care of it for me. Nothing's changed."

"Everything's changed, Mario."

"What, how? How, for chrissakes?"

"I am no terrorist, Mario."

It suddenly dawned on Mario what this meant.

"Oh, Christ, oh, mother in heaven, you're not going to do it, are you! I am dead. D'you hear me, I AM DEAD!"

Natalie came over to her father.

"What's this about, Dad?"

"Natalie, please . . ."

Natalie turned to Little Frankie.

"My father has been ill. He has only just recovered."

Mario gasped and bowed his head. Natalie took hold of him quickly and guided him to a chair. She turned to Little Frankie.

"Why don't you leave? Please leave!"

"Hush, Natalie. Please," Mario said, regaining his composure after a few minutes. He was breathing heavily. "I'm okay," he insisted. "Please, go upstairs."

Natalie looked at Little Frankie, then at her father. Finally, she went upstairs.

"I swear as God is my witness I didn't know who they wanted killed," Mario said. "I told them I could get the best. I'd heard about you . . . your reputation."

"Money? You owe them money, Mario?"

Mario nodded despondently.

"A lotta money?" Little Frankie said.

"Si!"

"So, who are they, Mario?"

"If I tell you, they will kill me."

"You'd better hope I get to them first. Who are they, Mario?"

Mario took a deep breath as if trying to make up his mind.

Finally, he said: "I do not know the bosses. I only deal with one person. He is minchia. You understand? The little prick! Marona mia, if I had money, I would pay to see him dead! Will you kill him for me? Okay, okay. His name. I'll give you his name. What the hell! Neville Ring. He runs a casino up west. The Twin Wheel in Soho."

Chapter 4

AT Paddington Station, Little Frankie opened a left-luggage locker and took out a package.

Later, in the privacy of his hotel room near Marble Arch, he opened the package. It contained a handgun, ammunition. and a shoulder holster. The gun was the one Little Frankie had ordered for the hit: a Smith & Wesson Model 36, .38 Chief's Special with a two-inch barrel. It weighed just 14 ounces and didn't ruin your suit. The Special was a favourite of his. And Little Frankie was not the only one who appreciated this compact, little gun. The cops liked it, too. It was for years a standard police weapon, favoured by many police agencies, including the NYPD.

Expertly, Little Frankie checked the gun thoroughly before loading the Special and placing it in the shoulder holster.

An hour later, Little Frankie found the front entrance to the Twin Wheel casino in Soho. It was early evening, and the casino was shut. He looked for another entrance.

Eventually, he found a kitchen door at the back of the building that was unlocked.

Once inside, he moved away from the kitchen and along a dark corridor. A large, young man appeared from nowhere and blocked Little Frankie's way. This was Fat Phil, one of Neville Ring's men.

"Yeah, mate?" Fat Phil said. "Who are you and what the fuck d'you want?"

Little Frankie ignored Fat Phil and went to pass him.

"Ere, where the bleedin' 'ell d'you fink you're going?" Fat Phil yelled.

He made a grab for the hitman. Little Frankie punched Fat Phil hard in the face. He rolled back like a big balloon and fell over, blood pouring from his nose. Little Frankie drew the Chief's Special and leaped on Neville Ring's heavy. He placed the barrel firmly under one of Fat Phil's red cheeks.

"Now, fat boy. Where's Neville Ring?"

"Office . . . end of the 'all," Fat Phil said, staring wildly at the Chief's Special.

"Show me."

Little Frankie let Fat Phil up, then holding the gun to his head, shoved him along the dark corridor. After a few minutes, they reached a closed door.

"Go in."

Fat Phil knocked. A voice shouted: "Come in!" Fat Phil opened the door and went in first. Neville Ring's office was a sparse room, located below street level. The pavement could be seen through a slit of a window.

Neville Ring sat behind a desk the size of a Cadillac. He was spiv-smart, typical East-Ender made good, right down to the shiny suit and Havana cigar. He was writing something down and did not immediately notice Little Frankie behind the enormous form of Fat Phil.

"Yeah, what is it?" Ring said without looking up.

"Uh, boss, you gotta see this!"

Now Ring looked up. Little Frankie turned Fat Phil so that Ring could see him and the gun he was holding.

"What the hell?"

"Down, fat boy . . ."

Little Frankie kicked Fat Phil so that he collapsed at the knees. Ring tried to get to his feet.

"Siddown!"

Ring sat down, his Havana cigar hanging limply from his lips.

"You know who I am?"

"Should I?"

"A half mil says you do."

"He's the bloke, Nev. You know . . ."

"Shut it, will you! Why the shooter, mister?"

"Are you the contractor?"

"The contractor? What kind of a question is that?"

"Are you?"

"I act for another party, let's say."

"Who?"

"That's their business."

"That's just it. It's not business. It's terrorism. So I am making it my business to find out who they are."

"Hang on a minute. You've lost me. Does this mean you're not going to honour the contract?"

"Right."

"You are dead meat, matey! They'll have you killed."

"They?"

"And they'll top me while they're at it!"

"You know the name of the people who ordered the hit?"

"I might."

"So, tell me."

"No way!" Ring said, jumping up. "What is this, anyway? I was told you was the best hitman money can buy. Do you know what Mario said? He said you was the ace of assassins! Don't make me laugh! Who does it matter who the bleedin' target is? For half a million quid, I'd do it meself."

"You might have to."

"Oh, you mate, are history!"

"And you will be right now if you don't siddown!"

Ring sat down again. Little Frankie threw Fat Phil forward on his face. He put his foot on the back of his neck and pointed the Special at Fat Phil's head.

"Oh dear, oh dear!" Ring said. "We have got ourselves in a right lather, haven't we."

"I'll ask you once. You don't answer right, I start shooting, capiche?"

Ring remained cocky. Mistakenly, he thought Little Frankie was bluffing.

"I want to talk to the people you talk to, so tell me now!"

"Well, I'm not tellin' you sweet FA, matey. How d'you like that?"

Little Frankie shot Fat Phil dead. The sound of the gun going off in that claustrophobic room was like rolling thunder. But the execution did the trick. Its ferocity shook Ring to the core. He fell back into his chair as if he had taken the full impact of the bullet himself. Then he sat there, staring in disbelief, like a limp, rag doll, muttering.

"Oh, Jee-sus Christ! Why did you have to do that?"

Little Frankie turned the Special on Neville Ring.

"Okay . . . Okay . . . Don't shoot, please God. I'll take you to someone!"

The vermilion red Bentley Continental - the one Little Frankie had seen earlier that day in Tottenham Court Road - swooped out of the casino and accelerated away through Soho.

Neville Ring was at the wheel with Little Frankie beside him, cradling the Chief's Special. Ring had not regained his composure since witnessing the shooting of Fat Phil. He was ghostly white with fear.

Chapter 5

THE red Bentley Continental paused at the gates of a country mansion, Harrington Hall near the Oxfordshire village of Homily. The gates to the mansion opened and Neville Ring drove in.

The Bentley pulled up on a gravel drive outside the mansion's front door. Ring and Little Frankie got out. Little Frankie had the Special in his right hand. He tucked the gun into his jacket pocket. Someone had seen them arrive and opened the door.

Meanwhile in London, at the Twin Wheel Casino, two of Neville Ring's men -- the red-haired driver of the Bentley Continental who had earlier given Little Frankie the Jiffy Bag, and whose name was Poppy, and another Ring goon, Danny -- struggled from the casino's back door into the carpark. They were carrying the body of Fat Phil wrapped in a carpet.

Poppy and Danny loaded the body into a dark-blue Rolls-Royce limousine. They dumped Fat Phil in the wide floor space in front of the car's rear seats. Poppy went back inside the casino, while Danny got into the Roller on the driver's side. Poppy returned carrying a shovel and a heavy canvas bag.

It was Peter, a Filipino butler in a tight black waistcoat that showed off his huge shoulders, who opened the front door of Harrington Hall to Neville Ring and Little Frankie. Peter led Ring and Little Frankie through the gloomy great house. A thought struck Little Frankie: it wasn't that Harrington Hall had seen better days, just happier days.

"What is this place?" he said.

"Harrington Hall," Neville Ring said. "Owned by - to give him his full monicker - Lord Reginald Homily-Harrington. Better known by one and all as Lord Reg -- lord of the manor, prominent member of the House of Lords and friend of the rich and powerful. Lord Reg is who I talk to . . ."

"It goes higher?"

For a moment, Neville Ring was his old, cocky self.

"Maybe a lot higher than you can reach, Yank!" Ring said with a sneer.

The dark-blue Rolls-Royce limousine streaked along the motorway in the fast lane with Danny at the wheel.

"Take it easy, Danny boy! You'll get us nicked," Poppy said. "That would be very silly with Fat Phil in the back, wouldn't it."

"But Nev said we was to get rid of Fat Phil A.S.A.P."

"Yeah, and we're doing it, right. But Nev weren't himself."

"What d'you mean?"

"Nev's in trouble, stands to reason. Think about it, Danny. Nev calls us, says get down the Twin pronto and take care of Fat Phil. No detail, mind you. Just get down here -- blah, blah -- and take care of it. He's off somewhere with the Yank, he says. But he wasn't supposed to see the Yank, let alone go anywhere with him. None of us was. That was the deal, Danny."

"Yeah?"

"Yeah," Poppy said. "Anyway, I reckon Nev was tryin' to tell us something without getting himself shot, if you know what I mean. So, when we've dumped Fat Phil, we're going to find Nev."

"But we dunno where he is."

"Maybe. But I know where I'm gonna start looking."

Peter the butler, Neville Ring and Little Frankie stood before huge double doors leading to a drawing room in Harrington Hall. Peter knocked on the door. A voice within boomed: "Enter!"

Peter led the way in. Lord Reg, a crimson-faced man, stared at them from a wheelchair across the room. His personal secretary, Eric Harbinger, was close by. Lord Reg was a bulky man with a booming voice to match. He was a no-nonsense, gentleman farmer of some significance and wanted everyone to know it.

"Ah, Ring! Come in, come in. Thank you, Peter, that will be all."

The butler, Peter, left quietly closing the huge doors to the drawing room behind him.

"You said it was urgent, Ring," Lord Reg boomed. "So get on with it, man! Who have we here?"

"My, er, associate, Lord Reg."

"Your associate, Ring?"

"That is, er, our associate, my lord."

"Our associate? What are you babbling about, man? I've never set eyes on this man before!"

Lord Reg's personal secretary, Eric Harbinger, leaned forward and whispered discreetly in his master's ear.

"What's that, Harbinger? What's that you say?"

"I believe this man is our associate, party to the, er, contract."

Harbinger, Little Frankie reckoned was a sharp little rodent. He twigged right away what was going down. Harbinger whispered once more into his boss's ear.

"All right, Ring, I understand," Lord Reg said at last. "But I was told there was to be no formal contact."

"He made me bring him here, your lordship."

"What?"

"He's gotta shooter, m'lord."

"A what, Ring! And for God's sake, man, stop calling me m'lord. You're not up before the bloody beak!"

"Sorry, m . . .er, Lord Reg, but he's gotta gun."

"So, what's the purpose of you coming here?" Lord Reg said turning to Little Frankie.

"It's quite simple your, er, lordship: I don't take the job."

No one said anything for a few moments.

"What? But my dear fellow," Lord Reg said with a thin smile. "As I understood it, there is a binding contract."

"I was asked to take care of some business. For my boss's cousin. Nothing much. Routine. But now I know this is not the case. This is much, much more."

"The money? Is it the money?"

"Jesus, this is not about the money! Who do you people think I am, some kinda goddam terrorist?"

Lord Reg turned menacingly to Neville Ring.

"Well, Ring?"

"How was I to know the geezer gets a bleedin' conscience, my lord?"

"But you said, leave it to me, your lordship, I'll get the right man, your lordship, you don't have to worry, your lordship!"

Again, Harbinger whispered in his master's ear. But he was waved away. Lord Reg moved his wheelchair menacingly towards Ring.

"Now, take it easy, your lordship. Calm down."

"Calm down? CALM DOWN! You bloody imbecile, Ring! I entrusted you with this crucial part of the operation. The people we are dealing with aren't idiots, you know."

"And who might they be?" Little Frankie said.

"I beg your pardon?"

"The people you deal with. Who are they?" Little Frankie said waving the Chief's Special at Lord Reg.

Lord Reg stared at Little Frankie and Neville Ring in turn.

Trying to be helpful, Ring said feebly: "He says, my lord, that he is going to stop it happening."

Lord Reg poured a cold look over Little Frankie which the hitman returned with triple venom. Lord Reg backed off.

"My dear chap, obviously you have no idea what these people are like. The people I am, let us say, answerable to."

"Try me."

Ring chipped in: "You can't stop this happening, Yank. Who do you think you're dealing with, a bunch of amateurs?"

"I'm afraid Ring's right. Your reluctance will merely hinder the process. I'm sure they will not allow you to get away with this "

"Damn right they won't," Ring said with nervous grin.

Little Frankie took a moment.

"Okay, so I can see we have a situation here," he said. "So help me out. You see, I never fail to carry out a contract. But this one is different. Someone in this room has gotta tell me who to talk to. If you do not help me, then believe me you are all on very thin ice. Very thin ice . . ."

"He's not bluffing, your lordshi. . ."

"Oh, for God's sake, Ring, will you shut up!"

"No, believe me, your lordship, this guy does not bluff."

Lord Reg began to backpedal his wheelchair. Harbinger was right beside him.

"So we have reached something of an impasse . . ." Lord Reg said.

"Shut him up, Harbinger," Little Frankie said.

"I beg your pardon?"

"You heard, pal. Use your pants belt and tie him up. Ring, you gag him." Lord Reg started to protest.

"I'm warnin' you to shut him up, Harbinger. Or I will."

Ring moved fast. Harbinger, though flustered, followed suit. Soon the sweating, swearing Lord Reg was bound and gagged.

Chapter 6

THE dark-blue Rolls-Royce limousine, with Poppy and Danny on board, pulled up on a deserted stretch of a half-built motorway spur road. They worked feverishly to drag the heavy body of Fat Phil wrapped in a carpet out of the limo. They didn't need to dig a hole. They simply rolled the body into a deep pit excavated earlier that day by a JCB mechanical digger.

It was surprisingly easy, in these circumstances, for Poppy and Danny to get rid of a body. The two villains took bags of cement from the back of the limo, smashed them open with a shovel and poured them into the hole on top of Fat Phil's body. Then they slopped in two large jerrycans full of water. Finally, the pair booted loose earth in on top of Fat Phil and got the hell out of there.

With Danny at the wheel, the Rolls-Royce thundered back along the motorway in the fast lane in the opposite direction to which it had just come.

Meanwhile, at Harrington Hall, Lord Reg was still fighting the inevitable, rock 'n' rollin' back and forth in his wheelchair. Little Frankie stepped up and tapped him with the Special to shut him up. Harbinger protested angrily.

"Oh-my-God, why did you d-d-do that? There's absolutely no need for violence. No need at all."

Little Frankie walked past Ring towards Harbinger. As he did, he pushed Neville Ring down onto a sofa.

"Now, Harbinger, you have to cool it, okay. And you have to tell me what this is all about. Do you wanna drink?"

"N-n-no thank you. I'm all right, thank you."

"Okay, then, tell me everything."

In a country lane above Homily village, the dark-blue Rolls-Royce limousine pulled off the road.

Poppy and Danny got out. Poppy took a canvas bag from the boot. He opened the bag to reveal two pump-action shotguns.

Within ten minutes, two dark figures emerged from the woods above Harrington Hall. Poppy and Danny were each carrying a shotgun. They moved silently across the mansion's lawns.

In the drawing room of Harrington Hall, Eric Harbinger appeared to be about to tell all to Little Frankie.

"Oh, my goodness, yes, er, where to begin . . ."

"I'm lissenin', Harbinger," Little Frankie said.

"Well, Lord Reginald has, since the 1970s, mortgaged every asset he has simply to stay on here. His dream has been to ensure that a Homily-Harrington remains in this house, esto perpetua."

"Excuse me, Harbinger?"

"Latin, sir. The Latin meaning forever. Well, literally it means: may it be everlasting! I exercise a certain amount of licence because the language is a mere hobby."

"Yeah, Harbinger? Jesus! Can we continue, please."

"Certainly, sir. In the early Nineties, Lord Reginald loaned his hertofore good name to a multi-million-pound building project to be carried out, we were told, in the Middle East. We'd considered many means of survival here at the hall: a wildlife park, golf course, and conference centre -- all of those predictably tiresome things. But they all needed huge investment and the competition was horrendous. This scheme, though, seemed to be the answer."

"It went wrong?"

"The recession. What else? It took us, that is, Lord Reginald and Homily-Harrington Hall, to the very edge of the abyss."

"We got done up, didn't we, like bleedin' kippers," Neville Ring added helpfully.

"You were in on this?"

"We was all in on it, weren't we! Lord Reg was a regular at the Twin and offered me some of the action."

"Mario Scallion?'"

"Small beer," Ring said, with some disgust. "Gambling's his thing. He owed a lot of dosh to a lot of people, me included. He bragged his big shot cousin, the mafia boss, would help him out."

"Lord Reginald and, er, Mr. Ring were part of a syndicate that collapsed," Harbinger said.

"One minute I was the sole owner of the Twin," Ring said bitterly. "The next I was out and running it for someone else."

"And these people are the same people who put out the contract, right?" Little Frankie said.

There was a deafening roar as two shotguns were discharged simultaneously from outside in the gardens. The drawing room's French window, which opened onto the garden, exploded, showering the room and everyone in it with wood splinters and glass shards.

Chapter 7

LITTLE Frankie was the first to react. Even before Neville Ring dived to the floor and Harbinger dragged the unconscious Lord Reg out of the way, Little Frankie had rolled fast across the floor towards the drawing room's main door.

Half-way across he checked himself and fired a few rounds from the Special through the hole where the French window used to be. This was followed by a lot of shouting from outside in the garden. Danny burst into the drawing room through the French window hole, blasting wildly with his shotgun.

Little Frankie put a neat bullet hole between Danny's eyes. Danny went down but Poppy was harder for the hitman to nail. Poppy concentrated on keeping Little Frankie pinned down behind a sofa near the door of the drawing room. Little Frankie had to get out. He glanced across at the smouldering French window. He waited until Poppy had to reload his shotgun before sprinting across the drawing room and diving through the remains of the French window.

Little Frankie tumbled across a wide stone terrace. He went all the way over the edge and fell into a rose garden. Rose bushes broke his fall but their thorns tore into his red Versace jacket.

He did not stop but crawled away quickly across the lawn into the welcoming darkness. Then he got up and ran bent double for the safety of a wood. One last wild shot from Poppy's shotgun went harmlessly over Little Frankie's head.

A dazed but livid Lord Reg was wheeled on to the terrace by Harbinger. Lord Reg stared murderously into the night. For a few moments, he was too angry to speak. Then he bellowed: "Quickly, Harbinger, inside! Get me that blasted mobile phone of yours."

Little Frankie holstered the Chief's Special and started walking away from Harrington Hall down a leafy lane lit only by moonlight.

In a short while, he reached the village of Homily, which was part of the Harrington Hall estate. The village was classically English, with a village green, a pub, a church, a shop, a post office, and a traditional red telephone box. Little Frankie went into the telephone box to make a call.

"That's right, Mikey, Homily in Oxfordshire. You got it?"

"Yeah, yeah, here it is. Hell, it's not far. I should be there in an hour, tops."

At Harrington Hall, Peter, the enormous butler, carried the body of Danny wrapped in bath towels down the steps from the main entrance to the Hall and placed the corpse in the boot of the dark-blue Rolls-Royce limousine. Peter retreated back into the house.

Neville Ring and Poppy emerged a few minutes later through the same door. Ring climbed into his red Bentley Continental and drove off. Poppy followed in the blue Rolls-Royce limousine. The cars drove down the drive and out through the main gate of Harrington Hall.

Mikey O'Callaghan, at the wheel of his 1970s Nissan Bluebird saloon, arrived in Homily to pick up Little Frankie.

Little Frankie and Mikey staked out Harrington Hall. Mikey parked his battered Nissan in an estate gateway fifty yards from Harrington Hall's main entrance. In the yard at Harrington Hall, Eric Harbinger loaded Lord Reg and his wheelchair into a specially converted Mini estate.

A few minutes later, the Mini estate, with Harbinger at the wheel left Harrington Hall. Little Frankie and Mikey followed Harbinger in the Nissan.

In the small hours, at a big, deserted roundabout over a motorway, a white American Lincoln Continental stretch-limousine was parked up with its lights off. The Mini estate, driven by Harbinger, arrived, and parked behind the stretch-limo. Harbinger carefully unloaded Lord Reg and his wheelchair.

Harbinger pushed his boss to a position beside the stretch-limo. Across the roundabout, Little Frankie and Mikey arrived in the Nissan. Mikey parked up, turned off the engine and killed the lights.

They watched as Lord Reg had an animated conversation with the occupants of the stretch-limo through a lowered, dark-tinted window. Suddenly, Lord Reg exploded in anger and a shot was fired from the stretch-limo. Lord Reg recoiled from the shot and he and his wheelchair went over. Another shot was fired from the stretch-limo and Harbinger ran for his life back to the Mini estate, leaving Lord Reg sprawled and not moving beside his upturned wheelchair.

Chapter 8

INSIDE the Nissan Bluebird, Little Frankie yelled at Mikey.

"Go, Mikey, go!"

Mikey started the Nissan and stabbed his foot down hard on the accelerator. Little Frankie drew the Chief's Special and rolled down the window as the ancient Nissan squealed its way around the roundabout towards the stretch-limo.

Harbinger, meanwhile, made a quick U-turn in the Mini estate and sped away. But the Lincoln stretch-limo was also quick off the mark for a big car. Its driver slammed the car into reverse and set-off at breakneck speed before swinging the stretch-limo around the right way to chase Harbinger.

As Harbinger in the Mini estate passed Little Frankie and Mikey – coming from the opposite direction in the Nissan – for a split second, Nissan and stretch-limo came face to face.

Little Frankie noticed that the Lincoln flew a white flag on top of its radiator grill. He let go a stream of firepower into the oncoming stretch-limo. Catching its occupants by surprise, the Lincoln veered off and plunged down the first available exit from the roundabout.

The Nissan continued on the roundabout until it arrived at the spot where Lord Reg lay beside his wheelchair. A few moments earlier, Harbinger had pulled up in the Mini estate. He had already jumped out and gone to the aid of Lord Reg.

"Help me! I can't stop the bleeding," Harbinger yelled. "Help me, please."

Little Frankie and Mikey also did their best to help Lord Reg, who had been shot in the neck.

"You have a cell phone, Harbinger? Er, a mobile?"

"Yes, sir, but the police?"

"If you don't call an ambulance, your boss will die."

Harbinger, in tears, made the call. After a few desperate minutes had passed, between them they managed to stem the flow of blood and Lord Reg, though barely conscious, wasl alive.

Little Frankie tapped Harbinger on the shoulder.

"Come on, Harbinger, who were those guys?"

"I'm afraid, sir, there's nothing you can do."

"What d'you mean?"

"The assassination is going ahead anyway."

"When? Where? Come on, you don't owe these people anything? They just shot your boss."

"But you cannot stop it happening, sir! It's this weekend . . . tomorrow, in Venice. The ambassador is on a private visit."

"You know exactly where and when, Harbinger?"

"Yes, sir, I do."

Chapter 9

ARRIVING at Venice's Marco Polo Airport the following afternoon Little Frankie was met by Giorgio 'Joey' Santoreggia, who was also known as Joey the Wheel. Joey was the son of a cousin of Little Frankie's boss, Don Salvatore Savoria. Joey was there to assist Little Frankie.

Joey the Wheel drove Little Frankie away from the airport in his car, a nondescript Fiat saloon.

"It's there, in the glove, Frankie, just like you ordered."

Little Frankie opened the glovebox and took out a package. Inside, was a neat double-action Beretta, Model 20, the smallest of the modern range, together with an ankle holster and ammunition. Little Frankie checked the gun, loaded it, strapped on the holster to his right ankle and packed the Beretta.

"Hey, Joey, this is for you. To show my appreciation, and Sal's."

Little Frankie stuffed a wad of notes into the glovebox. Joey handed Little Frankie a piece of paper.

"Thank you, Frankie. You need me, you call. I'm around until tomorrow night. That's my cell phone. Call me for anything."

Joey the Wheel dropped Little Frankie at the water bus depot. As he waited to catch the bus across to Venice, he was met by a man who introduced himself as Martin Koons, one of the American ambassador's aides.

"Hey, good of you to come, Mr er, Beloved?" Koons said. "That sure is one helluva unusual name, if you don't mind me sayin'."

"Call me Frank."

"Sure, Frank, let's go. This your first time in Venice?"

"Yeah, Martin, this is my first time."

Little Frankie and Koons started walking towards the water bus.

"Well, Frank, your first time is the best, believe me. I mean I could've got a private launch because these people have a whole fleet at their disposal. But we are going to take the vaporetto – because in this city the water buses are the finest way, trust me to take your very first look at Venice. This will allow you to see more of the city as you pass."

"You ever thought of becoming a tour guide, Martin? You seem to know what you are talking about."

Koons stared at Little Frankie for a moment as if he was not sure if the new arrival was making fun of him.

"Hey, Frank, you from New York?"

"That's right, Martin."

"Which part?"

"Brownsville -- East New York in Brooklyn."

"So, what makes a kid from Brownsville -- East New York in Brooklyn, go into journalism, Frank?"

"Why, Martin, I wanted to travel."

Koons said nothing for a few moments.

"Hey, you are some kidder, you know that, Frank!"

"Yeah, Martin, let's catch the bus." Little Frankie and Koons took their seats in the water bus and gradually, as the night drew in, they were themselves drawn into Venice's unique, dark beauty.

By the time the vaporetto arrived in the city, at Piazza S Marco, it was a wonderfully clear night. After disembarking, Little Frankie and Koons walked along the piazza towards a very large yacht.

"Mikey O'Callaghan is an old pal," Martin Koons said. "But I haven't seen your by-line, Frank. Beloved is not the kind of name I would miss, if you see what I mean."

"I'm what they call a commissioning editor, Martin. Only now and then they let me out. It's my turn to get off my ass and do some legwork."

"Well, I promised Mikey I'd take care of you, and I will, Frank. But I can only get you ten minutes tops with the ambassador. This is supposed to be a private party."

Chapter 10

THEY arrived at the large yacht, the Erica. Partygoers were queuing to get onboard. Little Frankie scanned the boat from bow to stern. He noticed the Erica was flying a white flag, like the one he had seen earlier on the Lincoln stretch-limo at the roundabout shooting.

"Some boat, huh, Frank? 4,000 tons, a crew of 75, 60 double suites -- one just waiting for you, Frank -- gym, saunas, swimming pool, casino, library, even a goddam greenhouse!"

"Yeah, who owns it?"

"You really don't know, Frank?"

"Nope."

"Well, it's owned by Nathaniel Publishing Inc., who just happen to own Alasdair's, yours and Mikey's magazine."

"What's with the white flag? I seem to have seen that someplace before."

"It's a kinda, er . . . an organisation. Forget about it."

Koons turned away abruptly from Little Frankie and pushed to the front of the queue of partygoers. Koons and Little Frankie were allowed on board straight away by the heavies guarding the yacht's gangway. But as Koons and Little Frankie climbed the gangway, there was a massive explosion aboard the Erica. To their left, a cabin was blown out across the dock.

"What the fuck?" Koons yelled. "Oh, my God! Oh, my God!"

Koons launched himself up the gangway. Little Frankie stayed right behind him. But while they were trying to get on the yacht, suddenly there were a lot of people trying to get off the Erica.

On deck people were fighting to reach the gangway and get to safety. Somehow Little Frankie stuck close behind Martin Koons. The pair barged their way through the crowds.

Once free of people, they hurried across a main deck and ended up in a deserted ballroom. Three men crossed the dance floor towards them. One, a tall, steel-grey-haired man might have been a mature movie star -- the kind women love in high-profile TV soaps. This was Robin I Locust III, American Ambassador to the Court of St James, in London, the royal court that formally receives all ambassadors accredited to the United Kingdom.

Robin Locust was flanked by two secret service agents. Martin Koon's relief at seeing his boss alive was palpable. But recognising Koons, one of the agents turned his gun on him and fired, killing him instantly.

Little Frankie dived for cover and rolled away, at the same time reaching for the Beretta in the ankle holster. By the time he looked up, the agents seemed to have forgotten about him and were busy bundling Ambassador Locust through an exit from the ballroom. Little Frankie jumped up and ran after them.

Instead of taking care of Ambassador Locust, the agents appeared to be kidnapping him, dragging him along between them.

"No, not the fuckin' gangway!" one agent screamed into a walkie talkie. "I wanna boat, starboard side of the bow, now! We are coming out, y'hear!"

"What about him?" the other agent yelled back at the one with the walkie-talkie.

"What about him? We finish right now what we should have done with that bomb."

He raised his gun to shoot the ambassador in the head.

"We shoot the mother . . ."

But Little Frankie was quicker and shot the agent dead. The other agent whirled around but Little Frankie dropped him, too, with a single shot.

Ambassador Locust sank to his knees. Little Frankie checked that both agents were dead. He again noticed the pure white flag emblem -- this time worn as lapel badges by both agents.

"Okay, Mr. Ambassador, we have to move. Stay close to me." Without a word, Ambassador Locust followed Little Frankie.

At the Erica's gangway, Little Frankie and the ambassador joined those people who were still streaming off the boat. As they waited their turn, the ambassador leaned in close to Little Frankie.

"Why shouldn't I call for help? You wouldn't shoot me, would you?"

"I'm not here to shoot you, Mr. Ambassador. But if it comes to a choice between you and me, believe me, I am the one who lives. Does that answer your question?"

Ambassador Locust nodded and even appeared to smile. He was a patrician. A diplomat of great prestige with a background of solid old American money. He was a cool customer even when faced with real danger.

A few minutes later, Little Frankie and the ambassador stepped off the gangway onto the dockside and hurried away from the burning Erica. They walked to the furthest water bus, which was the least crowded, and got on board.

The water bus pulled away from the Piazza, where the emergency services were now in full cry. Ambassador Locust sat calmly staring ahead. Only when they were clear of the city did he deign to speak to Little Frankie.

"Now, whoever you are, are you going to give me some kind of explanation?"

"An explanation as to why your own guys are trying to waste you? Uh-huh, no . . . You and I are from different worlds, Mr. Ambassador. I hear you are a personal friend of the President of the United States. You are a favourite dinner guest of the British Prime Minister and English royalty. Whereas me, I am the kinda guy whose idea of a good time is a weekend in Vegas. I am not gonna explain nuthin', Mr. Ambassador . . ."

"Yes, but you do seem intent on helping me."

"That bomb was for you, pal."

"Possibly. But there were bigger prizes on board: politicians, tycoons, princes even."

"All I can tell you is that I have to get you back to London. It's personal."

"Personal? To whom may I ask?"

"Personal to me, Mr. Ambassador. Who else?"

Chapter 11

AT the mainland water bus station Little Frankie hailed a cab to take them to Marco Polo Airport. At the airport, Little Frankie and the ambassador got out of the taxi and went into the terminal. The hitman found a payphone and made a call. Ambassador Locust stayed close by.

"Yeah, Mikey, I pulled him off the boat as his own people were trying to ice him. What? Okay, I'll ask him." Little Frankie turned to the ambassador. "You have your passport, Mr. Ambassador?"

"Yes, I do."

"Yeah, he has his passport. We'll get a plane back to London as soon as we can."

"No, I was going to Paris!" interrupted the ambassador. "I see no reason why I should change my plans. Besides, I have people there I know I can trust."

Little Frankie thought about this for a moment.

"Okay, Mikey, we're going to Paris. I'll call you from there."

Little Frankie hung up, then called Joey the Wheel.

"Yeah, Joey, lissen. I need you to get myself and another party to Paris tonight. Can you do that?" Little Frankie listened for a few moments. "Okay, yeah, good we'll see you there."

An hour later, Joey the Wheel, driving a white Mercedes, picked up Little Frankie and the ambassador outside the airport. From the airport they took the motorway to Milan.

After a short while, Joey said: "We gotta tail, Frankie." Joey stared into the rear-view mirror.

"What is it?"

"Red Alfa, couple of guys, with us since the airport, two cars back."

On the outskirts of Milan, Joey said: "Waiting to make his move."

"Yeah, I reckon," murmured Little Frankie.

"And here he comes!"

The red Alfa Romeo that had been tailing them came up fast behind the Mercedes. At that moment another car, a black Fiat, dived out of a side-turning, and forced Joey to swerve violently. A gunman in the Fiat let loose a stream of rapid fire at the Mercedes.

Little Frankie pushed Ambassador Locust to the floor of the car. He lowered the rear window and fired at the windscreen of the Fiat, hitting the driver. The gunman in the Fiat tried to return fire but the stricken driver slumped forward. The black Fiat swerved out of control and clattered into a row of parked cars before overturning.

The driver of the red Alfa stepped up his efforts to get closer to the Mercedes. But Joey was now in full flight, showing off his skills as a wheelman.

At a small private airfield near Milan, the Mercedes roared onto a runway and headed for a waiting plane, a small executive jet. Joey brought the Mercedes to a skidding halt beside the plane.

"Now, go, Frankie, go!" Joey yelled.

Little Frankie bundled Ambassador Locust out of the Mercedes. They ran to the executive jet where a man helped them on board.

Joey the Wheel clunked the Mercedes' automatic gearbox into drive. He spun the steering wheel and lined up the Alfa for a side-on collision. The rapidly accelerating Mercedes hit the Alfa a mighty blow in the nearside front passenger door and catapulted the smaller car onto its side.

From his seat in the executive jet as it began taxiing ready for take-off, Little Frankie watched Joey jump out of the Mercedes and finish off the two guys in the Alfa.

Little Frankie and Ambassador Locust sat beside one another in the plane. Apart from the man who had helped them climb onboard, the only other person present was the pilot.

"So what am I to make of you?" Ambassador Locust said. "Why would you help me, if, indeed, that is what you have been doing?"

"There is a contract out on you, Mr. Ambassador. I was hired to kill you and make it look like the work of terrorists."

"What are you telling me? That there is a conspiracy to kill me? You were hired to do it but you're here to protect me now instead? Am I supposed to believe that?"

"Believe what you like, pal, it's the truth."

"Who would want to remove me? And for what purpose?"

"They, whoever they are, want you out of the way. I don't know why. But I am not gonna let them do it."

"If you have my interests at heart, why not let my people take care of things?"

"Yeah, sure, like they were gonna take care of you all right, Mr. Ambassador, back there on the boat! You trust your people in Paris?"

"Yes."

Little Frankie said nothing.

Chapter 12

THE executive jet landed at a small airport outside Paris. Little Frankie and the ambassador were greeted by a driver in a large, black Citroen XM saloon. Soon, they were heading into Paris. Little Frankie and Ambassador Locust sat in the back.

"Can I call my friend?" the ambassador said.

"Now?"

"There is one colleague in particular I can trust. I can call him."

"Okay, but not from the car. We find a payphone."

The driver found a payphone and a few minutes later, Little Frankie and Ambassador Locust were crowded inside it. The ambassador talked briefly then hung up. He and Little Frankie left the payphone and went back to the Citroen XM.

"My friend won't meet me at the embassy but in the Bois de Boulogne at six."

Little Frankie looked at his watch.

"Okay, we have an hour. You know this place?"

"Yes."

Just before six o'clock that evening, in Allee de la Reine, Boise de Boulogne, Little Frankie and Ambassador Locust waited in the Citroen XM. Another Citroen, a grey Xantia estate with smoked glass windows, cruised by, slowing down as it passed the XM. One of the Xantia's front windows hummed down and a face half appeared. Then the window snapped shut and the Xantia rapidly pulled away. Inside the XM, Little Frankie turned to the ambassador.

"Was that your man?"

"I don't know. I couldn't see him clearly."

Before Little Frankie could stop him, Ambassador Locust was out of the car. He walked around the back of the XM and started waving at the Xantia, which had turned around in the broad road and was now heading back towards them.

"Is that you, Mitchell?" the ambassador yelled. "Mitch, it's me, Rob Locust!"

By now, Little Frankie was also out of the XM. Instinctively, he bent down and drew the Beretta from its ankle holster.

In the next second, Little Frankie saw a rear window of the Xantia hum down to reveal a black gun muzzle.

"Jesus Christ!" yelled Little Frankie. "Geddown, Mr. Ambassador, geddown!" He launched himself at Locust, at the same time firing the Beretta at the oncoming Xantia.

Little Frankie had done just enough. He and the ambassador fell together in a heap on the sidewalk as strafing Uzi sub-machine gunfire from the Xantia missed them by inches.

Instead, their car, the XM, was peppered with bullets. The Xantia accelerated hard away. Little Frankie helped Ambassador Locust to his feet. Then the hitman ran to the XM and wrenched open the driver's door. The driver was dead -- a bloody mess. Little Frankie grabbed hold of the ambassador and frog-marched him away from the scene of the shooting. The ambassador was no longer a cool customer but a man in deep shock.

As Little Frankie and Ambassador Locust hurried along Allee de la Reine, police sirens could be heard in the distance.

Ten minutes later, in a back street, Little Frankie broke into a Peugeot. He hotwired it and he and Ambassador Locust took off.

At a farm north of Paris, Little Frankie dumped the Peugeot in a yard. They switched to a tatty Citroen van.

Later, some miles further north of Paris, the old Citroen van pulled into a roadside services car park. Little Frankie and Ambassador Locust got out and went inside.

At a payphone, Little Frankie called his friend Mikey O'Callaghan in London.

"According to the newspapers, Frankie, the ambassador is feared dead."

"Okay, Mikey, but we know he is alive and with me now. We are heading for Calais," Little Frankie said. He turned to the ambassador. "Meet us at . . . where the hell is it?"

"Dover."

"Yeah, Mikey, some place called Dover. Sometime early tomorrow morning, I guess."

"Okay. Look, Frank, how can I put this? Don't turn him over to the cops, okay. Not on the boat. This is a big, big story. Let me do it first. I am right on deadline but if I write it, it can be in this week's magazine."

"Whatever you say, pal. Talk later."

Chapter 13

AFTER a few hours' driving and waiting for a night ferry at Calais, Little Frankie and Ambassador Locust boarded a P&O cross-channel boat headed for Dover.

They found some lounge seats and settled down to get some sleep. That is, the ambassador closed his eyes, while Little Frankie kept watch. Early next morning they went for breakfast in the ferry cafeteria. Little Frankie had got hold of an overnight edition of the London Evening Standard left on board from the ferry's inward trip to Calais and spread it out on the table between them.

"Well, Mr. Ambassador, according to this paper, I am breakfasting with a dead man."

"I'm almost convinced of your conspiracy theory," Locust said. "But why kill me? Who will stand to gain from my death?"

"Who says you are alive or dead? This newspaper, the radio and, I guess, TV. Detail is sketchy because this paper was quick off the mark. But they do say you are believed to have been killed in a bomb explosion while visiting the Erica in Venice. So the average guy thinks you are dead, Mr. Ambassador, because the media says so. We get Mikey to write a story that says you are alive and then all those who said you were dead are gonna start sayin' you are alive again. That's how it works, believe me."

As the ferry docked in Dover Harbour, Mikey O'Callaghan was waiting for them. Little Frankie and Ambassador Locust climbed into Mikey's Nissan Bluebird and they sped off.

At a motorway service station, Little Frankie and the ambassador waited in the car while Mikey called his editor, MG "Mustard" Alexander, from a payphone in the carpark.

Little Frankie could see that his friend appeared to be having an argument with Alexander while on the phone. Finally, Mikey slammed down the handset in disgust and returned to the car.

Mikey clunked the Nissan into drive and they scuttled back onto the motorway.

"So, what happened?"

"I get through to MG, told him what I have and he says he cannot use it! And I yell, whaddya mean you can't use it? He says it's sensitive and I yell, what's sensitive? The world's press, I say will be chasing its tail writing stories that Ambassador Locust is dead when I know he's alive. It's a great story! A world exclusive for Alasdair's Magazine!

"So he says, how the hell do I know that the ambassador is alive? He is with me now, f'chrissakes, I tell Mustard."

"Well, Frankie, MG is real interested in this. He gets almost friendly, which is strange. He says come on in, bring the ambassador with you and we'll talk. And I say, what about my story I can phone it over? And MG says bring it in with the ambassador. He says he has to see the ambassador before he can decide on my piece. Well, I . . ."

"So do it, Mikey."

"Huh?"

"We go to your place. You write your story and I take it to your boss, but without the ambassador."

"Why not take me straight to my embassy in Grosvenor Square in London?"

"I'll tell you why not, Mr. Ambassador. Someone tries to blow you up; two of your own agents try to shoot you; some other guys try to run us off the road; your so-called friend in Paris, this guy Mitchell, almost gets you shot. You have to agree, Mr. Ambassador, someone wants you out of the way pretty bad wouldn't you say."

"Dammit, man, are you saying there are people in London involved in this so-called conspiracy to kill me? I don't believe it."

"The agents who tried to kill you onboard the Erica, were they from London?"

"No, no one with me was from London. I was under the protection of European embassy staff. But, dammit, they were working on the same side. I say again: why would anyone benefit from my death?"

"That I don't know, Mr. Ambassador. But I aim to find out because a lot of people want you out of the way."

Chapter 14

MIKEY O'Callaghan lived in an apartment block near the Thames in London. Inside his cluttered bachelor-pad, Mikey punched out his story on his laptop computer, while sipping a large mug of coffee and munching on a Danish. Little Frankie and Ambassador Locust sat nearby on one of Mikey's sofas drinking coffee.

An hour passed before Little Frankie stood at the front door of Mikey's apartment about to go out. He was holding an envelope that contained a printout of Mikey's story.

"Look after the ambassador, okay, Mikey. Don't let him leave. Here take this."

He offered Mikey the Chief's Special.

"Jesus, Frankie, I don't need a gun! You are the guy with the gun!"

"You let him go, you blow this story I'm taking to your boss."

"Okay, okay." Reluctantly, Mikey took the Special from Little Frankie and nervously put it in his jacket pocket.

Little Frankie hailed a cab, which, inevitably, got stuck in traffic. He jumped out, walked a few blocks, and disappeared down the Tube at Tottenham Court Road.

He was making his way through the white tunnels of the Tube when he heard the tune again, A Whiter Shade of Pale. Around the next bend Little Frankie bumped into the busker he had seen before in the Tube. He was playing the same tune, on the same old synthesiser.

Little Frankie slowed but could not stop. Instead, he dropped some coins into the busker's laid-out jacket. The busker looked even more doped up than before. He was on auto. He remained expressionless, oblivious, and played on.

Minutes later, Little Frankie emerged from the Tube and asked a newspaper vendor the location of the office building he was looking for.

After a short walk, Little Frankie entered a large office block. He passed a brass nameplate on a wall in the entrance that told him that Alasdair's Magazine was on the fifth floor.

He went up to the fifth floor and introduced himself to a receptionist, who was sitting behind a large, mahogany desk. She asked Little Frankie to wait outside M G Alexander's office nearby in an area of brown leather sofas and a glass-topped coffee table decorated with magazines.

After a few minutes, the receptionist flicked on an intercom.

"There is a Mr. Beloved to see you, Mr. Alexander. He says he has something for you from Mr. O'Callaghan."

"Uh? Okay, sweetheart, wheel him in."

Little Frankie was shown into MG Alexander's spacious office. It was dominated by an over-large executive desk set before a picture window with a panoramic view of London. MG 'Mustard' Alexander was a little guy, surprisingly young and sporting a moustache to make him look older. He was swamped by the luxury leather executive chair he sat in.

"All right, so where' n hell is he?" growled MG Alexander.

Little Frankie sat down opposite Mikey's boss in a chair designed to make him look and feel small.

"Who, Mikey?"

"Yeah, goddammit! O'Callaghan! Who the hell d'you think I mean? I got a magazine to run, y'know!"

"And you have a story of Mikey's to run."

"I have? Where?"

"Right here." Little Frankie tossed the envelope containing the print-out of Mikey's story onto MG's desk. MG Alexander put on expensive-looking spectacles.

"Well, now, what do we have here?" He read Mikey's article in silence for a few minutes.

"One helluva story! One helluva story! Goddam shame it ain't true. What's all this contract-killing shit?"

"It's true all right."

"A horse's ass it's true. You're sayin' Locust is still alive?"

"Ambassador Locust did not die in any explosion in Venice."

"Then where is he, Mr. Bee-lov-ed? You bring him and O'Callaghan to me and we'll see how this story stands up."

"The ambassador is safe, and he's here in England. Tell me, O'Callaghan ever feed you a bum story?"

"Nope. But this is different."

"How's it different?

MG Alexander exploded in anger and leaped to his feet.

"Hell, you think I have to justify myself to you! I don't mister, so you'd better haul your ass back to your buddy O'Callaghan and tell him if he wants to keep his goddam job he'll get the ambassador to me before tonight. You got that!"

Little Frankie calmly reached across the desk and, while eyeballing MG Alexander, took back Mikey's story.

"I have a real strong feeling you won't be running Mikey's story even if we bring in the ambassador. So I guess we'll take it, and him, elsewhere."

MG grabbed for a phone on the desk in front of him.

"The hell you will!"

The Beretta in Little Frankie's ankle holster was in his hand before MG Alexander could speak into the phone. At the sight of Little Frankie's gun, he hung up.

"What are you, some kinda hoodlum?"

"Sit back and shut up. I'm getting tired of hearing your voice."

MG sank back into his oversized exec chair. He looked like a small boy with a fake moustache. But he was not finished.

"You don't scare me, mister! I don't know what kind of scam you and O'Callaghan are trying to pull but whatever it is, it won't wash with me. Ambassador Locust is dead! You understand? And he is gonna stay dead, you son of a bitch!"

"So how come a good guy publisher like you is mixed up in this?"

"You wanna watch that mouth of yours, boy. Y'hear? I have friends in very high places. I have friends who wanna stamp out media vermin like you. What are you, anyway? Some jumped up hack like O'Callaghan! Well, mister, you are mixing with powerful people here. I know a lot of people in the Pentagon and the White House -- never mind the goddam President -- people whose time will come; people whose sole purpose in life is to look good in Alasdair's Magazine!"

"But who is trying to kill the ambassador and why?"

"What business is that of yours?

Little Frankie reached across the desk and grabbed MG by his tie. He hauled him, face-forward, onto the desktop.

"I am making it my business to chase down the guys who put the hit out on Locust. You got that." MG squirmed.

"Aw, come on, come on . . . All you have to do is bring Locust in here. Forget O'Callaghan, he's a goddam loser. You get the ambassador to me and I know people who will pay you a lotta money."

"How much money?"

"Goddam you!"

"Half a million bucks?"

"Hell, that's a lotta money!"

"It was the price on Locust's head. It seems fair that your people should pay the same amount to get him back alive."

A thought suddenly occurred to MG Alexander. It was such a large thought it nearly choked him.

"G-g-g-goddam! You're no journalist! You're the hitman they hired! You're the guy who took the down-payment then refused to do the job."

"Right. But who hired me, huh? C'mon, you know who . . ."

"I'll never tell you that, boy -- gun or no gu . . ."

There was a knock at the door. Someone called from outside the door.

"Mr. Alexander, this is security. You all right in there?"

Little Frankie leaned in silently and expertly tapped MG Alexander to sleep with the Beretta. MG flopped out cold in his exec chair.

Little Frankie moved around the desk and got behind the door.

"Yeah, come in!" he growled.

The door opened and two security guards came in. They approached MG's desk.

"You all right, Mr. A?"

Little Frankie pushed the door shut.

"Don't turn around, I have a gun and you guys don't. Put your hands behind your heads and get on your knees."

The security guards did as they were told.

"You guys feel brave then follow me. You wanna live, stay right where you are. I tell you I am in no hurry."

Little Frankie slipped the Beretta back into the ankle-holster and noiselessly left the room.

Chapter 15

AT a payphone half a block away from the Alasdair's Magazine office, Little Frankie called Mikey O'Callaghan.

"Damn MG! I knew he wouldn't play ball!"

While Mikey was busy cursing his boss, Ambassador Locust slipped out of the apartment.

At a payphone up the street, the ambassador made a call. After a few words, he hung up, and waited.

Meanwhile, inside the apartment, Mikey stood, holding the phone, staring blankly around the room. He realised Ambassador Locust had given him the slip.

"Oh, Christ, Frankie, I'm sorry. One minute he was here, the next . . ."

"You let him go?"

"I'm sorry, Frankie. It was while I was on the phone to you."

Not a hundred yards away from Mikey's apartment, a white American Embassy stretch limousine glided to a halt. A door opened and Ambassador Locust got in. The limo pulled noiselessly away.

Ambassador Locust stretched out in the limo. Boy, was he glad to be "home", he said to the man sitting next to him. At last he felt safe, he said. But the man next to him, Ed Rich, an agent from the American Embassy in Grosvenor Square, calmly turned to the ambassador and without a word plunged a hypodermic needle into his thigh. Ambassador Locust was out cold in seconds.

Later, Mikey O'Callaghan was driving Little Frankie across London in his Nissan Bluebird.

"I thought, where would he go? It has to be the American Embassy," Mikey said. "So I set up a meet this evening with this guy I know there, Ed Rich."

But at that moment, unknown to them, the American Embassy stretch-limo in which Ed Rich had earlier picked up Ambassador Locust was heading north on the M1 motorway. Ed Rich had stayed on in London while the ambassador was being taken to Scotland.

That evening, in a Mayfair hotel, Little Frankie, Mikey O'Callaghan and Ed Rich were perched on stools at the hotel's main bar. Ed Rich was an ex-Marine and talked tough. Little Frankie noticed that Rich had an enamel white flag badge in the lapel of his jacket just like the agents the hitman had encountered on the Erica in Venice.

Ed Rich was trying to draw a line under the attack in which he was adamant the ambassador had died.

"I am not saying I don't believe you, Mikey. I'm saying as far as we are concerned Ambassador Locust died in that explosion in Venice. Unofficially, because you are a friend, I'd say lay off this one. It's big. Mighty big. You have a good job with Alasdair's and you don't want to jeopardise that."

As they left the hotel later, Little Frankie and Mikey watched Ed Rich walk away in the direction of Grosvenor Square. He hailed a passing cab.

"Mikey, I'm going to stick with him a while. I'll call you."

Little Frankie hailed a cab, too and got the cabbie to follow Ed Rich's taxi across town. Ed Rich got out of his cab outside the same building where Little Frankie had met MG Alexander.

Little Frankie called Mikey on his mobile.

"What? Rich and MG?," Mikey said. "What's going on? Anyway, maybe I have got us a break, Frankie. I received a call from Lady Jenny Harrington. Yeah, she is Lord Reg's estranged wife. She says to get down to Homily right away, Eric Harbinger is going to tell us what's really going on."

Chapter 16

LITTLE Frankie and Mikey headed out of London in the Nissan. After leaving the M4 motorway at Maidenhead, they drove down country lanes towards Homily.

Half an hour later Mikey's Nissan pulled into the carpark of the Harrington Arms pub. A silver Mercedes-Benz coupe flashed its lights once on the far side of the car park. Little Frankie got out and walked over to the Mercedes. Lady Jenny Harrington opened the driver's side window to speak to him.

"Are you the American?"

"I guess."

"You have a name?"

"Not yet."

"Not yet?"

"You wanna talk?"

"Sure. To our mutual advantage, you understand?"

"No, I don't understand. Where do you want to talk?"

"Right here and now?" Lady Jenny said.

"All right."

Lady Jenny smiled and broke into a rasping New York accent.

"Hey, you have a problem with that? You wanna go someplace else?"

"What was that?"

"What?"

"What? What was that? The accent, that's what," Little Frankie said. "You from New York?"

"Close enough, soldier. Get in."

Little Frankie stepped back and looked at Lady Jenny for a moment, taking her in. Then he walked around the Mercedes and got into the front passenger seat.

"So now you have a name?"

"Frank. Frank Roseo. They call me Little Frankie."

"Okay, Frank Roseo. I'm Jenny. Lady Jenny Harrington."

"From New York?"

"Raised on Amboy Street."

"No kidding? On Amboy?"

"Yeah, Little Frankie, I kid you not."

"And you married an English lord!"

"Not bad for a Jewish girl outta Brownsville -- East New York, huh, Frankie?"

"I'm impressed. A different sorta American dream that came true."

"I used to ride the bus with my brother up Fifth Avenue," Lady Jenny said. "Then we also used to like to see those houses on Riverside Drive. I was excited by all that history of American wealth! All those handsome people. My brother hated their guts but I admired them. I made up my mind to be up there with them one day."

"And you made it."

"Yeah, but I also had some talent, y'know. For fashion and writing about it. That's how I met Reg. Like Mikey, I wrote for a magazine. I met Reg at a cocktail party. We had a big society wedding, Frankie. The works."

"But it went sour. You divorced?"

"No way. And never will be if Reg has his way. We separated officially a year ago, but he would die rather than let Harrington Hall figure in any divorce settlement."

"No pre-nup then?"

"No, we were kinda too much in love can you believe!"

"So how can we help each other?"

"I've already done my bit. I've persuaded that worm Harbinger to spill the beans: either he gives you and Mikey the full story, or I go to the cops and let them deal with it. After I separated from Reg, I had an affair with his chauffeur, Tom Buckthorn. He told me about Reg's meetings with MG Alexander of Alasdair's Magazine, and a guy called Ed Rich from the American Embassy. And Reg's close association with Neville Ring, a convicted fraudster. Harbinger knows I've got enough on Reg to have him investigated by the cops."

"So where do I fit in?"

"Harbinger told me about you. He says you're going to get the guys who shot Reg. He told me about Locust, the American ambassador. So I figured I'll help you and then you can help me get my divorce."

"Harbinger agreed to this?"

"Yeah, he's waiting for you up at the Hall."

"What can I say? I'll do what I can."

Lady Jenny gave Little Frankie a business card.

"Will you call me, Frankie? This is my apartment in London."

"You can count on it."

Chapter 17

LITTLE Frankie and Mikey drove to Harrington Hall. Harbinger greeted them at the front door. Once inside, he led the way up the main staircase.

"Lady Jenny says you have something to tell us, Harbinger," Little Frankie said as they climbed the stairs.

"Please bear with me, sir," Harbinger said over his shoulder. "Follow me."

At a landing, Harbinger continued to lead the way through the great, gloomy house to a master bedroom.

Once inside the bedroom they saw Lord Reg asleep, tucked up in a huge four-poster bed. The three men came up quietly to his bedside.

Harbinger was in despair, close to tears. His fear now was that Lord Reg might not make it.

"So there it is, gentlemen. Pulvis et umbra sumus ¬ we are dust and shadow. After all we have been through, all our sacrifices, these people shot Lord Reginald like a dog in the street."

"You had no idea what you were getting into, Harbinger?"

"How could we know? All Lord Reginald wanted was to stay on here. But if you are looking for revenge, then, as her Ladyship intimated, I will help you."

"I don't want revenge, Harbinger. I just wanted to stop the ambassador getting wasted."

"But if the agents who tried to kill him have him now," Mikey said. "Ambassador Locust might already be dead."

"I don't think so," Harbinger said. "If he didn't die in Venice then he will now be regarded as a prize, a bargaining chip to be cashed in later. Gentlemen, please let me explain."

Harbinger moved away from Lord Reg's bedside to the window. Little Frankie and Mikey joined him.

"Lord Reginald has an old friend, a Lord Skirret. They were at school together – Eton, of course. Lord Reginald always says after being at Eton one feels capable of anything in life. Lord Skirret thinks so. Nevertheless, he is clearly a fantasist.

"He dreams of taking real power – on a governmental level – and has a particular relish for the military. It is my guess that Ambassador Locust has been spirited away to Lord Skirret's Scottish estate from where I believe the final, pathetic act in this whole sordid affair will be coordinated.

"You see Lord Skirret is adamant that the finale is run from there because of the area's historical links. The Special Operations Executive -- Britain's secret saboteurs -- were trained in what is known as the Rough Bounds and at Arisaig for the final assault on Germany during the last war."

"So what, they are going to hit someone or something?"

"That I don't know," Harbinger said. "We were never privy to such intelligence. Lord Skirret boasts of some rather unpleasant connections with the United States. He flies a white flag from his car, the same from the battlements of his castle in Scotland. This is the symbol of an organisation called WhiteFlag."

"I've seen that flag . . . on the limo that tried to run you down, Harbinger. The agents in Venice had white flags as lapel badges and so, too, did Ed Rich."

"Precisely. These are supporters of WhiteFlag. Not all of them can afford to be so open. I've heard, gentlemen, that some have their nipples pierced and wear the WhiteFlag symbol on jewellery concealed from the outside world. But all are deadly serious about their affiliation. In America they hate government, believe the President is a wimp . . ."

"Yeah, what a can of worms 9/11 unearthed. WhiteFlag has right-wing connections in the States?" Mikey said.

"Lord Skirret openly admits to links with ultra-right-wing people there. His obsession is guns, something his lordship is an expert in. He freely supports the gun lobby in America in their fight against any federal ban on assault weapons. It is Lord Skirret's dream that WhiteFlag will become a globally connected organisation that is standing up to terrorism by fighting back."

"Sorta international vigilantes?" Mikey said.

"Precisely."

"But how in hell did Lord Reg get mixed up in all this apart from being at school with Lord Skirret?"

"Money. What else? Lord Skirret told Lord Reginald that these people would pay a considerable amount of money for his support in this country and Europe. A member of the House of Lords; a friend of Cabinet ministers; well respected in the City. Once Lord Reginald could see hard cash, he was theirs."

"But he was soon out of his depth," Mikey said.

Harbinger nodded sadly.

"So where is this place, Harbinger?" Little Frankie said.

Later, in Lord Reg's study, Little Frankie called his boss, Don Salvatore Savoria in New York City.

"How are you, Frankie? Someone said, only Little Frankie works on his vacation." The phone echoed with the Don's hard man laughter.

"I'm good, Sal. But I could use some help, padrino."

"Who do you want?"

"Vinnie Bugloss and Herman Chamomile."

"Okay. You got 'em. You need hardware?"

"It's organised."

"You want them soon?"

"Next plane out?"

"You got it. It's done. Oh, Frankie . . ."

"Yeah, Sal."

"You come back to us by the twentieth of the month."

"What's so special about the twentieth?"

"We have something to discuss, Frankie. It affects our future. I want you here, okay."

"I'll be there."

Chapter 18

AT London's Heathrow Airport early next morning, Little Frankie and Mikey O'Callaghan picked up their crew, who had just arrived from New York. Herman Chamomile and Vinnie Bugloss, carrying a minimum of luggage, climbed into a rented Volkswagen Caravelle people-carrier. With Little Frankie at the wheel, they wasted no time in heading north to Scotland.

Inside the VW, Mikey sat in the front passenger seat next to Little Frankie. Behind them, in the mid-way seats, were Vinnie and Herman.

"So Lill'l Frankie, you are tellin' me this guy Skirret is a lord and lives in a castle, right?" Vinnie said with a dopey grin.

"According to Eric Harbinger, Vinnie," Mikey said. "The guy we were telling you about, the Skirret family has lived there for centuries. It was the seat of the MacIains and later the Campbells. They held it for the King during Prince Charles Edward's rising in 1745."

"No shit, Mikey!"

"So, we are gonna raise some hell in a real-life castle!" Herman said. "Jesus, Frankie, it's good to be in England. I have waited for this opportunity for so long and I tell you for why, okay. Two years ago, I have to hit this Englishman. He comes to Vegas and with a broad they scam me. So, I have to whack them. They cheat me outta my money, y'unnerstand! So I whack the broad and this is easy. But when I go to ice the English guy, with my grandfather's Luger -- ja! that's funny, huh! -- it jams! I cannot believe it! The guy, who I learn is called Timothy, gets away. I chase him out of the hotel and what do you think, he gets hit by a fuckin' car, yeah! Well, Timothy is lying there in the road. I go over to him, lean over and ask him where the dough is from the scam. I say I need to know this right now, Timothy before I finish you off. What gets me is that he seems a nice guy. You know, Timothy has charm. Lotta charm. He keeps mumbling that his name is Timothy and he is a straight up and down guy and I say, to make conversation with the poor guy, all right, Timothy, call me Al. Then I say, where is the dough?"

"Al? Why Al, for chrissakes, Herman?" Vinnie said.

"I always wanted to be an Al. It is a good all-American name, don't ya think? More American than Herman! Anyway, this guy Timothy gets to me, okay. There is something about him. I like him. In other circumstances I think we could have been pals, okay! Then Timothy says, Al, the money I took is for my son. To get him through school in England."

"Hey, Herman but the guy was a scam artist!" Vinnie said, laughing.

"Sure but lissen, will ya! Timothy says the dough I am owed is all in this one place, this special place, in what he says is 'the Bank of the Isle of Wight'. Yeah, that's what he says, 'in the Bank of the Isle of Wight', here in England. All I have to do is take his wallet with his identification and deposit box details, come to England and collect. I reckon I get the son through school and keep the rest."

"You think the dough will be there, Herman? Bearing in mind the guy made his living from scams?"

"Hey, Vinnie, why would a guy lie with his dying breath?"

"Because that's how he earned his living, Herman," Little Frankie said. "The guy didn't know any better."

"Right," Vinnie said.

"Frankie, you don't think this guy was on the level?" Herman said. "I have a picture of the kid from Timothy's wallet and an address for the school."

"I heard of a guy who once used a picture of his grandmother on a hunnred scams," Little Frankie said.

There followed a few moments of silence.

Then Mikey said, very seriously: "Well, I've lived here for 20 years, Herman. And I don't want you to rain on your parade if you know what I mean. I'm sure England has a helluva lot of banks. And some of them might be in the Isle of Wight. But I'm pretty damn sure none of them are called the Bank of the Isle of Wight!"

There was absolute silence in the VW while this sank in. Then everyone, including Herman, cracked up and started laughing.

The VW Caravelle people carrier sped on its way, next stop Scotland.

Chapter 19

SEVERAL hours passed before Little Frankie was able to drive the VW Caravelle through magnificent Glen Coe towards Fort William, in the Scottish Highlands. After Fort William, they continued their journey north round Loch Lochy towards Invergarry. It was a breathtakingly clear evening in the Highlands.

At around dusk the VW Caravelle pulled into the carpark of Mountain View Lodge. Little Frankie, Mikey O'Callaghan and Little Frankie's crew, Herman and Vinnie got out of the people carrier and went inside to check in.

The Lodge dated back to the 16th Century. Modernisation included log cabins in the grounds for tourists. After checking in, Little Frankie parked the VW outside his log cabin and everyone settled in for the night. Later at a bar in the Lodge, Little Frankie was having a nightcap, a Scottish malt whisky, which he found as enjoyable as any American bourbon, his usual drink. He was asking the barman if he knew any guides.

"If you're looking for someone who won't gossip," the barman said, "'Gypsy' Benjie Borage is your man. He's a tinker and knows these hills better than anyone. Pay Benjie a tidy sum and he'll act as your guide."

"Where do I find this guy?"

"Just around the river bend. About 200 yards. Turn right outside the door. You'll see his caravan."

Little Frankie and Mikey took a walk along the riverbank. As they approached Benjie Borage's caravan across a dewy field, the tinker had seen them coming. He came out to meet them.

"Ye want to go ower high?" Benjie said.

"Excuse me?" Little Frankie said, bemused.

"I've gotten the best heid in the countryside. Canna ye look after yisself braw and weel?"

"Jesus!" muttered Little Frankie.

"You'll take us over, right, Benjie?" Mikey said.

"Aye, sair. I've had a braw life travellin' the hills but 'tis verra difficult if ye're na used to it."

Mikey turned to Little Frankie.

"He'll do it, Frank. Give the guy some dough."

"Uh? Okay. How's a hunnred grab you, pal?"

"One hundred pounds!" Mikey said. "We'll pay you one hundred pounds!"

"Och, naw!"

"Two hunnred!" Little Frankie said.

"Noo, noo sair, ye dinna understand," Benjie Borage said. "Ye'll do no siccan thing. I couldna spend a hundred poonds in a month o' Sundays up here. I'll taek ye for fifty."

"Did I hear right, Mikey? We got the guy for fifty?"

"Yeah. I'll bet you never had one like this before, eh, Frank."

"Okay. Fifty pounds. Deal!"

"Thank you, sair. Ye'll want t'go inna mairnin'?"

"Yeah. What time?"

"Bes' be starting early. I'll meet ye inna burn yonder a' six."

Benjie pointed to a footbridge thirty yards from where they were standing.

"Ye'll be passin' thrae the Skirret estate?"

"Yeah, I guess. Is that a problem?"

"I'm oftener on this saed. But I been up thair last back-end and I saur some dour deevils runnin' aboot. An' they wairnt stalkin' naw beasties!"

"Soldiers, Benjie? Were they soldiers?" Mikey said.

"Nae tellin', sair. 'Twas mairn wi' green breeks and brown jackets. And rifles, though they wairn't stalkers, I'll warrant. Was one I knae. He's sometimes a gillie for Laud Skirret. He comes frae the Lawlands and has a verry shairp tongue. I was oot on the hill, mindin ma business -- they could baith see me nor hear me -- yet this one taeks up his club an' says for me to clear away."

"But you'll still take us?"

"Oh, aye, I'll taek ye, sair. I'll see ye in the mairnin'."

Little Frankie and Mikey walked back to their log cabins.

"Hey, Mikey, that's one helluva language."

"Can you imagine the conversations Benjie and Herman are gonna have!"

Chapter 20

EARLY next morning, Benjie led Little Frankie, Mikey, Herman, and Vinnie up a track towards, in the distance, the Arrowhead Mountains.

The evening before Herman and Vinnie had hired hiking equipment for everyone from a villager recommended by the hotel. Now the crew, Little Frankie and Mikey were equipped with waterproof anoraks, hiking boots and rucksacks with a change of clothes, some food and guns.

The latter, Uzi machine guns and Glock handguns, had arrived by courier in a package organised by a Savoria family contact of Little Frankie's in Glasgow.

Benjie had his customary small rucsack and leaned on a crooked stick. He also had a small mongrel dog called Willow by his side.

Later that morning with the sun continuing to shine, Little Frankie's party reached the top of a pass that had a spectacular view across the surrounding valleys. Benjie raised his stick and swept it across the view.

"Glen Lovage. And Loch Gale an' yonder's ta Fam'ly. Acts laek a fairbeck to'un castle. Natural protector, y'ken? The Fam'ly hills are near Skirret land an' so's the lach and thairn forests. I'll taek ye doon past tha lach an' inta the Fam'ly hills where ye can taek a look at Skirret Castle an' tha estate. But watch out for Laud Skirret's mairn. If'n ye see any, tell Benjie."

A few hours later Little Frankie and his crew were walking along Loch Gale, with Willow the dog bounding ahead of them.

There was the sound of gunfire in the distance. Willow came running back to his master's side.

"What's that, Benjie?" Little Frankie said.

"Dog sin somethin', sair. Could be summa Skirret's men onna shoot. Or tha dour deevils I was tellin' ye aboot. Best stick close and ke'p quiet." Little Frankie's party emerged at the edge of a forest. Benjie signalled them to get down. They all lay on their fronts. Little Frankie scanned the hillside with binoculars.

He spotted half a dozen men in battle fatigues racing down a hillside to a main footpath. Then the men moved away.

"Any idea who they might be, Benjie?"

"I'll taek a wee look. Bide ye here like stones."

Benjie set off, accompanied by Willow.

A short while later, they returned.

"I've naer sin the laeks of it, sair. Poor auld bitch offa hind riddled with bullets up yonder. Na for sport auw f'meat, I'll be bound."

Little Frankie said: "The guys we saw were carrying assault rifles – M16s – which means they're probably hunting something other than deer. We don't want to meet up with them unless we have to, Benjie."

"I sed I'd taek ye ower and I will. We'll strike up higher and come down onna deevils." After another hour of walking, Little Frankie and his crew got their first view of Skirret Castle. They lay down on their fronts again in a hollow high above Loch Lovage to take in the view.

Immediately below them, at the edge of Loch Lovage, was Skirret Castle. It was ancient but in good repair. The castle sat on a rock at the edge of the loch, joined to the mainland by a jetty but easily cut-off from the jetty by a drawbridge.

The castle had four towers and a helipad between the towers. Two helicopters were parked on the helipad. Jutting out across the loch was another, longer jetty, with smaller mooring jetties coming off it, as if someone was establishing an upmarket marina in the heart of the Highlands.

There was an assortment of boats moored at the jetties but not pleasure cruisers, more a mix of military craft. Across the loch there was a disused boathouse and broken-down jetty. On the far side, a trickle of an inlet joined the loch to the sea beyond. In the far distance were the black dots of the Western Isles.

Through his binoculars, Little Frankie could see white flags flying from each of the imposing four towers of Skirret Castle.

"WhiteFlag!" Little Frankie said in a fierce whisper.

Chapter 21

"A REAL-life castle by the sea!" Vinnie said.

"That's one helluva place to get into, Frankie," Herman said.

They all watched in silence for a while. There was a lot of activity around Skirret Castle.

"You know, Mikey, this is kinda weird," Little Frankie said. "It takes me back to 'Nam."

"You got called up in '69 when you were 18, right, Frankie?"

"Right. Those choppers down there are Huey Cobra gunships; I counted five LCUs, Utility Landing Craft, on the jetties, just like the ones we used in Huey; those guys were carrying M16s; I wouldn't be surprised to see a coupla M4B tanks and a fleet of Ontos."

"A lot of stuff got left behind after the pullout from Saigon in '75," Mikey said. "Billions of dollars' worth of stuff -- apparently, even a goddam main frame computer -- just left for the gooks. And no one knows what happened to it. Not the arms dealers, or the Government agencies. They were all asking: what happened to the arms left behind in 'Nam?"

Little Frankie turned to Benjie, their guide.

"Is there some place we can hole up, Benjie?"

"If ye're stayin' tha nicht, there's a wee hut ower yonder. 'Tis used by walkers and the laek."

"Okay that will do nicely. You have any idea how we can get into the castle unnoticed?"

"Now thair's a question, sair. 'Tis not ma place to ask questions but with all those deevils runnin' aboot doon thair, an' wha' with the guns an' the laek, I've half a mind not to poke ma nooze. Ye're noo the pooleese, are ye?"

"We are no more the cops, Benjie, than you're a Texas Ranger," Mikey said.

"But we need to get inside that castle," Little Frankie said.

"Maeks no diff'rence to me, sair, as long as ye're noo the pooleese. 'Tis a lang while since I was in th' castle. Skirrets are singular people an' noo mistaek. Tha wee Skirret hisself is noo laeked around here. Seldom seen since his father was kilt on holiday abrard an' the bairn became t'laud. On t'other saed of tha castle is'n entrance -- an ancien' sooridge outlet inta the lach. Ye'd need a boot -- laek a wee punt. Ye culd get unda the grill in a loo boot, y'ken?"

"But this entrance may not still be there?" Mikey said.

"It main't not, sair, as ye say. But 'twas thair for mairn centuries past."

"We'll try tonight," Little Frankie said.

Later in the mountain hut where they planned to stay for the night, Little Frankie and his crew ate a meal of meat and rice, cooked by Benjie. Then it was time for him to go.

"Reckon I best be on ma wey," Benjie said.

Little Frankie peeled off a fifty-pound note and a twenty-pound note from his roll and gave the money to Benjie.

"I know you said fifty," Little Frankie said. "Take it, you've earned it!"

"Thank ye, sair. Will ye be able to get yisselfs back doon?"

"We have a map," Mikey said, optimistically.

"I'll taek a look up this wey tomorra," Benjie said. "'Tis no trouble. Auld Willow laeks the exercise. Good nicht t'ye."

Chapter 22

LIKE commandos on a mission, Little Frankie, Mikey, Herman and Vinnie darted along the night skyline above Skirret Castle then disappeared. They reappeared, cutting down the hillside towards a broken-down boathouse on the opposite side of the loch to Skirret Castle. They paused for a second or two. Then, they all ran to the back door of the boathouse.

Little Frankie poked a rusty padlock with the butt of the Uzi sub-machine gun he was now carrying. The lock fell off. When he pushed it open, the door half-disintegrated. They all went inside.

What once must have been a wonderful place in an idyllic spot was now filled with junk, dirt and dust. Everything in the boathouse -- holed punts piled high, deckchairs, wooden-slatted sun-loungers -- was brittle to the touch. Only a Canadian-style canoe slung from canvas straps from the rafters looked watertight. Herman and Vinnie cut it down and dropped it into the water.

"Okay, me and Mikey go inside," Little Frankie said. "Herman, you and Vinnie stay put here. If things look bad, I want you to create a diversion."

"What you mean Frankie, hit the boats?" Vinnie said.

"Raise hell, Vinnie!" Little Frankie said. "Hit the boats, the choppers, anyone or anything. We're up against Skirret's private army here." In the dead of night, a canoe slid across Loch Lovage towards Skirret castle. Little Frankie and Mikey, on their knees, moved slowly, using ancient wooden paddles to scoop out the water and propel the canoe forwards.

Finally, they let the canoe drift and after some minutes located the entrance to the castle through a sewer and waste pipe that Benjie had described to them. By lying flat in the canoe, they scraped under a grill. Little Frankie and Mikey and their canoe then disappeared into blackness.

Lit only by torchlight, Little Frankie and Mikey inched along until the tunnel appeared bigger and lighter. The darkness gave way and the canoe emerged into a brightly lit area. This looked newly built: there were bright white tiles on the walls, and a newly installed walkway and handrail ran along one side of the tunnel. There were piles of building materials that looked recently abandoned. There was a sharp bend in the tunnel thirty yards ahead.

"Quick, out!" Little Frankie said. "We have to ditch the boat!"

They pulled alongside the walkway and climbed over the handrail. Little Frankie grabbed some bricks from the pile of building materials and holed the canoe. They watched it sink. Then they moved off cautiously along the tunnel's walkway.

Finally, they reached an open space, an underground mini loch beneath Skirret Castle. In shape, it mirrored Loch Lovage. In scale, it was a fraction of the loch's size. The walkway Little Frankie and Mikey walked along, continued on around the whole of the mini loch's perimeter. On the far side, where the walkway widened into a dock, Lord Skirret's soldiers were gathered. They were standing before a platform bathed in light. Above the platform, giant white flags drooped in the airless space.

Little Frankie raised his binoculars to take a look. He saw three men on the platform. They were all wearing white battle fatigues, the kind worn by commandos in Arctic conditions. Little Frankie recognised one of the men -- the publisher of Alasdair's Magazine, MG 'Mustard' Alexander.

"Your boss, MG is one of those guys, Mikey."

"Goddam!"

"One of the other guys must be Lord Skirret," Little Frankie said. "Let's get closer."

Outside the castle, two boats, a cutter and a launch, came into Loch Lovage from the sea. The cutter stood off while the launch came in very slowly towards the main jetty. Two of Lord Skirret's soldiers, both armed with Uzis, walked warily along the jetty. The launch continued to approach the jetty. A man on the launch addressed the soldiers on the jetty through a megaphone.

"We are Her Majesty's Customs & Excise officers," he said. "We would like to come ashore."

Chapter 23

INSIDE the castle Little Frankie and Mikey were working their way around the mini loch. Eventually, they got close enough to hide among oil drums and within hearing distance of the platform.

MG Alexander tapped a microphone to speak.

"Gentlemen we are at war!" MG Alexander shouted to cheers. "We are at war with the goddam wimps -- those liberal idealogues who want America to roll over and die. We have been led into this abyss by a long line of wimps for presidents, including President George W Bush. Yes, yes, yes, we have! You know it . . . And I can assure you, I know it! I know it! (He shouted above the noise of wild cheering.) "And . . . And . . . ANNNNND! They wanna take away our guns! Yes, yes, they do. Can you believe it! (The soldiers roared their disapproval.) They wanna take away our guns! So what are we gonna do about it? What are we gonna do about the mamby pamby UN, G7, GATT, the goddam financial in-sti-tu-tions, that damn Brady bill and successive governments that support a federal ban on assault weapons? And what in the hell, gentlemen, are we gonna do about terrorists who have the nerve to pull off something like 9/11? What are YOU gonna do about it, gentlemen? I'll tell you what I'm gonna do. I am gonna HIT BACK! (roaring cheers) Yeah, yeah, yeah, I am. I am. I am gonna hit these motherfuckers where it hurts! Are you gonna do that? Are you? Are you? ARE YOU?"

Skirret's soldiers chanted, "YEAH! YEAH! YEAH!" and continue cheering MG Alexander.

"During the Renaissance the white flag was used in Western Europe to indicate surrender. We gentlemen have turned that on its head. Our white flag means attack (cheers) attack! Attack! (resounding cheers).

"We are gonna keep on hitting them until we break 'em down. Yeah, yeah, we break 'em down. And what do we hit them with? Yes, what do we hit them with, gentlemen? We hit them with . . . WWWWWHITEFLAG!"

The shouted word resounded around the mini loch amid frenzied cheering and stomping of feet from Skirret's soldiers. For those guarding the castle outside the visit from Customs officers was totally unexpected. The launch containing the officers was close to the jetty. The two Skirret's soldiers waiting for them had no idea how to handle the situation. Except by force.

"Supposin' we don't want you ashore, pal?" shouted one of the soldiers.

"Yeah, take a hike."

"We have the authority . . ." the Customs officer began to say through the megaphone.

"Yeah, well this is the only authority around here," shouted back one of the soldiers.

He fired a burst of automatic fire at the launch. It ripped the Customs officer with the megaphone off the bow of the launch and into the water. There was a moment's hesitation but then, with a roar of its engines, the launch took off. Skirret's men sent a hail of bullets after it.

Within moments there was covering machine gun fire from the Customs' cutter, standing by in Loch Lovage. More of Skirret's men ran onto the jetty and began firing at both the launch and cutter. Herman and Vinnie, who had been watching the action with interest from their vantage point in the boathouse, exchanged glances. Without a word, they started shooting at Skirret's soldiers. Then a Skirret soldier ramped things up by firing a Soviet-made RPG-7 rocket launcher at the cutter.

The only racket inside the castle's mini loch was the continuing thunderous applause for MG Alexander. He waited for the cheering to die down.

"But first . . . but first, gentlemen, I want you to hear from the man who has made all this possible. I give you . . . your commander-in-chief, Lord Skirret!"

Skirret's soldiers increased their applause and cheering once more for Lord Skirret, a small man who blinked continuously in the spotlight that fell upon him as he stepped up to the microphone.

"Thank you. Thank you, my good friend, MG Alexander. And thank you, gentlemen. You've heard our mission, a European mission, let's say, that will be coordinated from here during these next months. Our mission is code-named Ultra2, which makes me particularly proud. My father was one of a group of brilliant British academics who put together a crude computer at the Code and Cipher School at Bletchley Park during the last war to break German codes. The codeword for this vital work was Ultra and, gentlemen, it helped win the Battle of Britain."

Murmurs of approval from Skirret's soldiers, most of whom were too young to remember any war.

"And the very soldiers who spearheaded the fight back against Hitler were trained here, at my ancestral home, on this estate. So you can see we have a lot to live up to. Only now the enemy is a different kind. The enemy is terrorism, the kind that humiliated all Americans in New York City on September 11 and is no doubt planning more attacks on both sides of the Atlantic. This is a threat to us all, gentlemen, but we can do something about it. And that is why you are here. But to business . . . It will be incumbent on us to coordinate your ops from here but we also felt we needed let's call it a mobile headquarters that could watch over you when you are in the field. So, gentlemen, we've come up with this . . ."

The lights dimmed around the mini loch. The spotlight swung away from the stage to the middle of the mini loch which began to bubble and gurgle.

Little Frankie and Mikey strained forward from their hiding place for a better view. Piped military-style music was played loudly from hidden speakers.

"You think their secret weapon, Frank, is the Loch Ness Monster?" Mikey whispered.

"What the hell is that?" Little Frankie said, not taking his eyes off the bubbling water.

A full-size submarine rose up slowly and dramatically out of the water. Skirret's men went wild with delight, stomping and cheering. The piped music faded away.

"Gentlemen, this was originally a Russian-built submarine," Lord Skirret said, taking up the microphone once more. "In late 1968, this Golf Class Soviet nuclear submarine left Vladivostok and was heading towards Hawaii when a mysterious explosion sank it. The Soviets searched for it but to no avail. A bod in US Naval Intelligence -- eager no doubt to bone up on this class of Soviet sub for future SALT talks -- suggested a salvage operation. They knew where the sub was but the salvage costs were prohibitive, so the CIA was brought in. And so too was that enigmatic millionaire, Howard Hughes.

"The salvage operation -- codenamed Project Jennifer -- went ahead but was supposed to be top secret. The media got hold of the story -- and, for them, the magic link with Howard Hughes -- and eventually the CIA had to explain themselves. The CIA said the sub had been partially recovered. Another recovery operation began in the utmost secrecy. But in fact the sub had been fully recovered on the first mission and was in surprisingly good order. The CIA took what information it required from it then put it into mothballs. Lieutenant Colonel Terry Southern, formerly of the US Security Council, here . . ." Lord Skirret continued, introducing Terry Southern, the third man on the platform. "He persuaded the powers-that-be to sell it to offset the £152 million cost of the initial salvage operation. WhiteFlag bought the submarine with funds raised by donations and an international network of arms dealing. Anyway, enough, this is Precious and she will indeed be precious to you all as you go about your missions. Her crew are fully versed in the use of SLBMs, gentlemen, just the kind of back-up to provide you all with complete peace of mind."

Lord Skirret's monologue was interrupted by a deafening, screaming siren.

The sparkling image of order and triumphalism was torn up before Little Frankie and Mikey's eyes.

"What the hell?"

On the platform MG Alexander was shouting.

"Jesus Christ! A full goddam red alert!"

He grabbed the microphone from Lord Skirret.

"RED ALERT! RED ALERT! TAKE EVASIVE ACTION! TAKE EVASIVE ACTION! MOVE IT! EVERYONE MOVE IT NOW!"

Chapter 24

SKIRRET'S soldiers scattered and ran. The mini loch was in uproar. The siren continued at deafening, screaming fever pitch. Only Precious, the submarine, remained calmly stalled in the centre of the mini loch.

Mikey turned to Little Frankie.

"You think Herman and Vinnie started a war already, Frankie?"

"Let's take a look."

Little Frankie and Mikey moved quickly. They walked fast along the gangway in the direction of the platform. They hid as some of Skirret's men burst past them carrying MI6s.

Little Frankie and Mikey discovered steps to an entrance that would get them into the castle proper. But two of Skirret's soldiers had been posted as guards.

In the noise and confusion, Little Frankie went in hard. He drew his Chief's Special and shot one guard dead. The other made a run for it up the steps but Little Frankie nailed him, too. Little Frankie and Mikey dragged the guards out of sight and quickly changed into their white battle fatigues. Then they began climbing the steps that would take them into the heart of the castle.

Little Frankie and Mikey kept climbing steep, worn stone steps inside one of the castle's towers. Mikey, inevitably, was slower.

"Go ahead, Frank. Go ahead, I'll catch up," Mikey said stopping to rest.

Little Frankie kept going up until he came to a padlocked door. He drew the Chief's Special and shot away the lock.

Mikey shouted from below. "Jesus, Frank! Are you all right?"

"Come on up, Mikey."

Little Frankie kicked his way through the door and emerged on a platform on one of the castle's four towers. The view around him was spectacular. Mikey came puffing into view. Exhausted, he plonked himself down next to Little Frankie. The hitman was looking over the parapet watching the battle outside.

"What the hell goes on down there?" Mikey said, still out of breath.

"Some guys on a coupla boats out in the loch are firing on the castle. And Skirret's soldiers are firing back."

Mikey hauled himself up off the floor to take a look. He and Little Frankie took in the chaotic scene below them for a few minutes.

"Where's Herman and Vinnie?" Mikey said.

"I guess they were shooting from the boathouse. But that's on fire. I hope that's them up there in the hills."

"What we gonna do, Frankie?"

"Locate the ambassador."

"You think he's here or even still alive?"

"I'm gonna take a look. Stay put."

Little Frankie hurried back down the tower's steep stone staircase then headed for the mini loch. He realised he had to knock out the sub; cause maximum damage, add to the chaos. The mini loch was deserted by now.

Little Frankie found the oil drums he and Mikey had hidden behind earlier. One by one he rolled them over with a few kicks, broke their seals with the butt of the Uzi and pushed them into the mini loch. Oil began to spill across the surface of the water.

With the mini loch's surface near him swimming with oil, Little Frankie made a crude fuse from builder's yarn, lit it with his Zippo, tossed it onto the oil and retreated quickly. As he did, there was a flashfire across the mini loch followed by a mighty explosion.

Little Frankie made his way to the helipad. He found some steps and climbed onto a gallery overlooking the helipad. The three men who had moments before been bathed in glory ¬-MG Alexander, Terry Southern and Lord Skirret were shouting at one another beside a helicopter whose engine had a few moments before roared into life. Two of Skirret's men were holding Ambassador Locust nearby.

Without warning, Terry Southern screamed at MG Alexander and punched him to the ground. He shoved Lord Skirret to one side and moved to climb on board the helicopter. He was getting out. But not quickly enough. Little Frankie dropped Terry Southern with his first shot. The next two shots were for the men who were holding the ambassador. Everyone else scattered from the helipad as Little Frankie knocked out the helicopter pilot then drilled the chopper itself until it caught fire.

Little Frankie watched MG Alexander stagger to his feet, and, gun drawn, hustle Ambassador Locust away as the helicopter exploded. Little Frankie scrambled off the gallery to give chase. Little Frankie darted through the smoke-filled corridors of Skirret Castle in pursuit of MG Alexander and the ambassador. Now and then, MG stopped, turned around and fired a few shots at Little Frankie.

The magazine publisher hustled the ambassador through an open ancient door. But when he tried to close it behind him it would not budge.

By the time Little Frankie reached the door, MG and the ambassador had disappeared. Little Frankie followed them cautiously into Skirret Castle's Rose Garden.

Chapter 25

THE tranquillity of the Rose Garden was in stark contrast to the battle raging elsewhere in the castle and outside around Loch Lovage.

MG Alexander stood next to a quietly functioning fountain. He held a Glock pistol to the head of Ambassador Locust.

"Come on in, you son of a bitch," MG shouted. "This is the jerk you went out on a limb for." MG waved the barrel of the Glock in Ambassador Locust's face. "I have only one question, Yank. Why, f'chrissakes?"

Little Frankie walked slowly towards MG and the ambassador. He held the Chief's Special pointing downwards at his side.

"Tell me why you wanted me to waste the ambassador," Little Frankie said.

"What?"

"You wanted me to kill him to give you and your private army an excuse to go on a manhunt for terrorists."

"What was it? Not enough goddam money?"

"There was a reason, pal," Little Frankie said calmly.

"And what the hell was that?"

"Whatever else I am, I'm no terrorist."

"What are you then a goddam fool?"

Mimicking MG, Little Frankie said: "No, I ain't."

Little Frankie's gun arm rose like lightning. He fired a single shot from the Chief's Special. The bullet entered MG's forehead. His Glock went off wildly above the ambassador's head, as MG was lifted backwards off his feet by the impact of the bullet from the Chief's Special. MG's body flopped into the fountain.

Ambassador Locust collapsed, and fell on his knees, his head in his hands. Little Frankie walked over and helped him to his feet. Little Frankie went to the bottom of the steps of the tower where he had left Mikey.

"Mikey! Mikey! Get down here, we're getting out."

Mikey shouted back that he was on his way. Little Frankie, Mikey and Ambassador Locust picked their way through the castle. They emerged in the castle's main square. There was frenzied activity everywhere but mostly from Skirret's soldiers fleeing the castle. They were crowded onto the drawbridge trying to get out.

Overhead, two Customs & Excise helicopters circled with searchlights trained into the square. A megaphoned voice droned down from one of the helicopters with a stark message for the fleeing soldiers: "This is Her Majesty's Customs & Excise. Give yourselves up!"

Little Frankie, Mikey and Ambassador Locust joined Skirret's soldiers trying to get out of Skirret Castle.

As the soldiers filtered through the castle's main gate and across the drawbridge, there were still exchanges of fire between Customs officers and Skirret's men who had remained in the loch.

A Jeep roared up behind the fleeing soldiers at the main gate and tried to push its way through. Lord Skirret was on board the Jeep with his driver. Skirret stood up in the Jeep.

"Make way there! You men, let me through!"

Lord Skirret sat down. The Jeep's driver sounded the horn continuously. From a mass of soldiers' backs Lord Skirret saw one of his men turn and look directly at him.

"Fuck you, Skirret!" the soldier yelled, opening fire on the Jeep. The bullets shattered the Jeep's windscreen and several hit Lord Skirret in the face. His body bolted backwards in the front passenger seat and then he was still, his face shattered. The driver jumped out of the Jeep and ran away.

The Jeep was abandoned yards from the way out, with Skirret's soldiers surging around and past it.

Once outside Skirret's men scattered and took to the hills. Little Frankie, Mikey and Ambassador Locust followed suit.

Some soldiers were captured by Customs officers and elite back-up units from D11, but many disappeared across the moors and into the night.

Little Frankie, Mikey and Ambassador Locust met up with Herman and Vinnie and they climbed together to the top of one of the hills overlooking Loch Lovage. They watched as Skirret Castle burned below them.

A small dog appeared.

"Hey, it's Villow. You have come back to us, little fellow," Herman said making a fuss of Willow.

Then the tinker, Gypsy Benjie Borage, appeared as if by magic next to Little Frankie.

"Och, I knew tha dour deevils were up ta nae good. 'Twas frantic noises I heard way doon in tha glen. I couldna resist a wee laek."

"Skirret's dead," Little Frankie said.

"Aye, is that so? In that case, would ya laek me to show you the way back doon soon, sair?"

A few minutes later, they set off, Willow skipping ahead of the men.

Chapter 26

TWO days' later, at the arched entrance to Adam and Eve Mews, Kensington High Street, London, Little Frankie paid off a black London cab. He walked under the arched entrance and stopped. He stood in the cobbled street in gently falling rain, at one expensive-looking building. He walked to the front door of a mews cottage and reached out to push the doorbell.

But before his finger could touch the doorbell, the door opened. Lady Jenny Harrington came out to greet him.

"So, the soldier is home from battle," she said with a smile.

"What can I say?" Little Frankie said. "We won, I guess."

Lady Jenny's eyes suddenly filled with tears.

"You know you grow to hate someone you once loved . . . and when he's gone . . . like that . . ."

"His lordship ran outta luck, is all. He got mixed up with a bad bunch and he got shot and didn't make it."

"I think all he really wanted to do was to safeguard his family name. Surely, you of all people understand the importance of that, Frank."

"I guess. I'm sorry."

Lady Jenny tried to smile through her tears. She pulled Little Frankie close to her and then inside. The door shut with a click. In the first-class cabin of a 747-jet airliner somewhere over the Atlantic, Little Frankie sat back in his seat.

He was very happy to be going home. He wore headphones and was listening to the 1985 live recording in Modena of Luciano Pavarotti singing Mamma.

Little Frankie loved this recording in particular, not only for the song and the voice, but also to hear an ecstatic Italian audience. Little Frankie literally had his head in the clouds while Lady Jenny slept in the seat next to him.

A few rows back, Herman and Vinnie made merry with the champagne and the cabin staff.

Mikey O'Callaghan was there, too, chatting to Herman and Vinnie. Mikey returned to his seat near Little Frankie, who was still revelling in the music. He opened an eye when Mikey sat down. Little Frankie stopped the music and sat up.

"What date is it, Mikey?"

"Date? The date? It's the, ah, nineteenth. Why?"

"Sal wanted me back for the twentieth. A big meet, he said."

"Well, you're gonna make it, pal."

"I hope I make it Mikey."

"Frank, you are five hours ahead already. Time difference, remember?"

"What do I remember? I can't get used to those . . . what d'you call them?"

"Time-zones, Frank."

"Yeah, the time-zones."

"Makes the world go round, pal."

"Mmmm . . . Eastern Time!"

"Yeah, Eastern Time is what we are rolling into very soon," Mikey said looking at his watch."

"It's the one I know," Little Frankie said. "The only one I know."

"Yeah but now you have done Europe, Frank."

"Done Europe? What is done?"

"Done. Travelled around; visited Europe. You have been there."

"Sure, I've been there, Mikey. Shot at and still none the wiser."

"So, travel does nothing for you, Frank?" Lady Jenny said sleepily.

"All I'm saying is that I am none the wiser."

"You think Ambassador Locust was happy to be recalled to Washington, Frank?"

"Recalled, Mikey? To head the CIA? Are you kidding? I think there is one very happy man. Locust is ambitious. Very ambitious. He wants to go all the way. One day we might be saying, 'Hail to the Chief' to President Locust. And you could be interviewing him for the cover of Time magazine, Mikey."

"Hey, I'm just grateful I am out of Alasdair's."

"Well, you got your exclusive in the end, Mikey."

"Sure did. But now I am thinking I will go into TV. I've had offers, y'know."

"TV! TV?"

"Yeah, Frank. Tee-Veee!"

"Gee, Mikey, I'd like to see you on TV."

"What about you, Frank? You think your boss is gonna come up with something big for you?"

"Hey, whoa there Mikey! I have no idea. For a while, I thought this whole thing might go against me."

"How come?"

"I'll tell you guys something, shall I? My whole working life I never once failed to carry out a contract. Not once, you understand what I'm sayin'? Never! Word gets around, you never work again. Over! Finished! But this one – whichever way I looked at it – I could not, would not go through with it! It was a nightmare. I came over to England for a small vacation and it ended up a nightmare. Again and again, I say to myself of all the things I am – I am no terrorist. I am an American. I am a patriot. And I had to say no."

"And you were right to say no, Frank."

"I know that Mikey, and Sal knew it and all those guys who tried to take down Ambassador Locust – MG Alexander, Lord Skirret, all those guys from WhiteFlag – I reckon, eventually, they knew it, too."

"Forget about it, Frank," Lady Jenny said, touching his arm. "You have fulfilled all your obligations. You are home and dry."

"Yeah, home and dry!" Little Frankie said. "From now on, I stay put in New York!"

"Uh-huh . . . me, too!" Lady Jenny said, going back to sleep.

"Mmm," Mikey said. "And Vegas!"

"Yeah," Little Frankie said. "Not forgetting Vegas!"

"Still, that was some vacation, huh, Frank?"

Little Frankie smiled and looked across at his friend.

"Yeah, Mikey, that was one helluva vacation!"

Little Frankie sank back into his seat, closed his eyes, and listened again to the soothing voice of Luciano Pavarotti singing Mamma.

THE END
All rights reserved, Copyright © Nigel Wigmore 2024.

ABOUT THE AUTHOR

Nigel Wigmore worked as a journalist on The Guardian for more than two decades and a further decade on the London Evening Standard. He lives in the Cotswolds in England and writes a weekly column on cars. For illustrations and links visit browsingimpala at Instagram and for more books search Nigel Wigmore Amazon.

Printed in Great Britain
by Amazon